**A shot blasted, shattering
the desert silence.**

Raider and Doc flung themselves behind the boulder.
Slugs came down, singing off the rock.

"HEY YANQUI! WELCOME TO MEHICO!"

J.D. HARDIN

THE MAN WITH NO FACE

BERKLEY BOOKS, NEW YORK

THE MAN WITH NO FACE

A Berkley Book/published by arrangement with
the author

PRINTING HISTORY
Berkley edition / September 1983

ISBN: 0-425-06337-2

A BERKLEY BOOK ® TM 757,375
Berkley Books are published by The Berkley Publishing Group,
200 Madison Avenue, New York, N.Y. 10016.
The name ''BERKLEY'' and the stylized ''B'' with design are trademarks
belonging to Berkley Publishing Corporation.

PRINTED IN THE UNITED STATES OF AMERICA

CHAPTER ONE

Cradled by the claim "We never close," a large eye stared intimidatingly down at Doc and Raider from an upstairs window as they rounded the corner onto Fifth Avenue. The words PINKERTON NATIONAL DETECTIVE AGENCY framed both eye and stern assertion. The agency's offices, located at numbers 191 and 193, were well removed from Conley's Patch, the slums along lower Fifth Avenue, a straggling array of cheap saloons, pawnshops, bagnios, one-story shacks, and disreputable boardinghouses. Here, on the opposite side of the Chicago River, rose brick and stone buildings, citadels of commerce, bastions of business, fortresses of finance, the Windy City of the future taking shape.

Raider, born and reared on a bottomland hog farm in northeastern Arkansas, had seen Kansas City, Denver, San Francisco, and other cities in the West, but this was the first time in his life he had been east of the Mississippi. Chicago rendered him speechless. The height of the buildings, the endless flow of horsecars, hansoms, carriages, wagons piled with goods, vehicles of every type and description, the legions of pedestrians jostling one another, the unabating clamor set his mouth agape and his dark eyes protruding in wonderment. Gaping and staring as well were the Chicagoans passing him, unaccustomed as they were to the sight of a fellow human clad in copper-buttoned Levi's, holstering a six-gun in plain sight attached to a silver-buckled belt, supporting a full-rigged saddle with one shoulder, wearing a battered and dusty Stetson and well-worn Justin boots heeled with spurs with rowels that jingled merrily with every step.

1

Doc, at Raider's side, was impeccably attirred as usual. He was wearing a smartly tailored blue pin-striped fingertip-length four-button cotton coat with matching trousers. He sported as well a Pasha hat with silk ribbon, raw edge, and curling flange brim. He looked every inch the Chicago gentleman of means and enterprise. Anyone sighting this mismatched pair would immediately assume that one was escorting the other to the Dearborn Theater, there to place him on exhibition as a model of a frontier primitive, complete with Colt .45 and three-day beard. Fortunately, Raider took no notice of the stares, the titters, and the murmured comments directed at him by passersby, so absorbed was he in the sights and sounds of the big city.

Crossing the avenue, nimbly dodging traffic and gaining the opposite side, they mounted the stairs to the second floor of the agency. They were greeted by a ruddy-faced clerk whose weft foundation toupee was parted in the middle and dispatched hairs in opposite directions down the sides of his scalp. His glasses were set so tightly against his eyes his lashes dusted the lenses with every blink. His head was set in a shiny, starched collar like a pudding in a bowl. This specimen ushered them into a large office where two elderly, depressingly homely ladies sat side by side punishing identical Sholes typewriters. Neither typist lifted her eyes from her work as the two newcomers entered. Raider and Doc were shown to chairs. Raider set his saddle on the floor beside him and put one foot on it protectingly.

"Mr. Wagner will be with you shortly," said the clerk over his shoulder as he hastened back to his desk in the corner.

The new arrivals sat side by side, hats on knees, eyes occasionally wandering to the two typists, who seemed to be in a race to see which of them could get to the bottom of her page before the other. Here, mused Raider, lollygagging was clearly taboo. Allan Pinkerton paid his people to work, and work they did. Like galley slaves under the lash. Raider transferred his hat from one knee to the other, then back. He glanced at the drop octagonal clock on the wall over the clerk's desk. Twelve noon. Mealtime, advised his stomach, a rumbling reminder. He stood up, intending to cross to the window to look down into the street, but no sooner was he on his feet then the clerk turned and stared at him; the two typists stopped as one and stared at him. The hint registered; he sat.

A door opened and closed in the adjoining office. The voices of the two men who had come in were somewhat muffled, but understandable.

"Will, I don't care a hoot aboot exemplary records and past performances. What a mon does today ond tomorrow are what count. I shouldn't have to remind you thot the Ponnsylvania Railroad is perhops our moost important client, ond when Henry Govinner, one of their chief officers, coomplains aboot George Bangs, auld ond dear friend ond loyal ond hardworking officer of the agency though he may be, it's oor responsibility to take prooper oction."

Doc and Raider exchanged looks. The clerk scribbled furiously, one hand cupped over his ear in a vain attempt to shut out the voices from the other room. The two ladies pounded their machines with renewed fury.

"Ogain, listen closely," continued the voice of resentment. "Ahem, I hov joost possed Mr. Bangs on Third Street between Walnut ond Wellings Alley, droonk as a lord, reeling ond staggering from side to side, trying hard to retain a cigar in his mooth, sustaining himself from falling by wildly cotching all posts ond rails ond finally londing on a pile of building debris. He came oot of a saloon near Wellings Alley, nine A.M. Mr. Boyd informs me thot this is the second time Bangs has been seen in this condition."

"Who's Boyd?"

"Another official with the Ponnsylvania. We moost coontoct my son Robert ot once."

"I presume he's in his office in New York."

"See thot a copy of this telegrom is sent on to him ond onclose a letter ordering him to pay Bangs oop to Saturday. Thon he's to send him bock here by train. I'll take the motter from there. Noo, what's oll this fiddle ond fuss aboot thot scondalmonger Wilbur Storey?"

The door separating the two offices opened and in clomped Allan Pinkerton, his eyes fired with indignation, his face deeply etched with exhaustion and the illness that had been afflicting him for the past three years. His salt-and-pepper beard thrust forward like the cowcatcher on a locomotive, his ear tips were tinged with pink, and he seethed, inhaling and exhaling through clenched teeth. William Wagner, superintendent of the Chicago office, followed him in. He was half a head taller than his superior, stoop-shouldered, his fire-engine red galluses too tightly braced, lifting his trousers two inches up from his shoes. In his hand was the Pennsylvania Railroad official's telegram of complaint.

"Storey wants to hire us to shadow Lydia Thompson."

"Who, may I osk, is Lydia . . ."

"Thompson. She's the star of *The Black Crook*. It's playing at the Orpheum."

Pinkerton gasped. "Wilbur Storey cavorting with a stage player? I don't believe it!"

"He's not cavorting. He wrote a column in the *Times* implying the lady's a strumpet. Accused her of 'capering lasciviously' on the stage. Last night she hid in the bushes in front of his house and when he came home she jumped out and began thrashing him with a horsewhip. On top of which she's suing him for libel. He wants operatives assigned to shadow her. He wants to collect a bagful of dirt that he can throw back at her in court and force her to drop the libel suit."

"Pshaw! The mon's a Copperhead ond a domned fool to boot. He's olready made himself the loffingstock of the city. Better he crawl onder his desk ot thot foolish rog he calls a noosepaper ond hide his oogly face till the thing blows over."

"He's demanding we take the case."

"We'll do nothing of the sort. The agency does not hondle cases of a scondalous nature or divorce cases. We deal with crimes, robbery, ond murder, not trivial squabbles between artistes ond moodslinging scolliwags."

"Chief, Wilbur Storey wields a lot of power in this town.

The *Times* has the biggest readership in the state. Why make an enemy out of him?''

''Why not? I'd welcome the opportunity!''

Pinkerton swung around and for the first time noticed Raider and Doc, sitting with their hats still perched on their knees. His glance drifted to Raider's saddle, his eyes lifting in wordless comment.

''Weatherbee . . . Raider.'' He came forward, his meaty hand outstretched, his heavy shoes pounding the floor, jouncing the typewriters on their stands. ''What are you two doing here? The lost time I looked your location pins on the mop were somewhere oop in northern Montana. Great Falls, wosn't it?''

''I sent for them, Chief,'' said Wagner. ''If we could step back into your office I'll explain.''

Pinkerton spread his hands. ''Explain here, mon, we're amoong friends.''

''It's, ah, a matter of some delicacy.''

''Ah,'' countered the chief, scowling, stabbing an accusing finger at one then the other. ''In dootch again, is thot it? I might hov guessed.''

''Nobody's in dutch,'' hastened Wagner. ''Chief . . .''

The four retired to the other office. It was crowded with studded leather chairs, a long oak table, and a desk, set of all places in the center. The walls displayed photographs of well-known Chicagoans—the *Tribune*'s Joseph Medill, Deacon Bross, his associate, Cyrus Hall McCormick, Marshall Field, George Pullman, the renowned religious revivalists Dwight Moody and Ira Sankey; and, in the place of honor between the two windows overlooking Fifth Avenue, his likeness draped with red, white, and blue bunting, was President Abraham Lincoln. In the corner of the picture he had scrawled: ''To Allan Pinkerton, a most zealous and fearless patriot. Yours in admiration and gratitude for your many services, A. Lincoln.'' Photographs of Pinkerton operatives also graced the walls.

''Sit,'' barked the chief, depositing himself in his favorite chair.

"With your permission, Chief," began Wagner. Leaning over, he pulled open the top drawer on the right side of Pinkerton's desk. He produced two letters. The intercom box on the chief's desk droned insistently.

"Yes?" he asked, depressing a lever and lowering his nose to within an inch of the box.

The female voice at the other end mumbled unintelligibly.

"Damn!" exclaimed Pinkerton. "It's Storey. The nincompoop's out in the reception room, demonding to see me. You go, Will. Give him today's *Tribune* to dawdle oover. Let him see what a decent noosepaper reads like. Noo, wait, let me. I'll nip this nonsense in the bud. Con you imogine a grown mon being horsewhipped on his own front stoop by a slip of a girl? Stay put, you two, I'll be bock in two shakes."

He left. Wagner held up the two envelopes, handing one to Raider, the other to Doc. They took turns reading each of the letters.

"Jayhawker Justice," murmured Doc.

Raider nodded. "Kansas."

"A third one came just this morning." Wagner patted his shirt pocket. "I haven't shown it to the chief yet, but it's the same story."

"What has the agency been doing in Kansas lately?" asked Doc.

Wagner shrugged. "Nothing special, not in the past two years. The Clancy gang, the ones referred to in both those letters, were actually apprehended in Ogallala, Nebraska. They tried to rob a Denver & Gulf train; it was carrying a good-sized shipment of gold under heavy guard. Two of the guards and a brakeman were killed, and all six Clancys collared. They've got 'em in the pen in Lincoln awaiting trial. They've been tried and convicted and they're sure to be hanged, but their lawyers have gotten it put off and put off. Governor Garber's had his hands tied with red tape. But these notes suggest whoever the Clancys' friends are they're getting worried; they see time running out."

Doc read the third note. "They're threatening to kill the

chief if Garber doesn't pardon the gang. This bunch must be half-witted.''

"Half-witted or not, they'll kill him if they get the chance.''
Wagner had been leaning against Pinkerton's desk, his arms folded; now he straightened and began pacing.

"We, the staff, both his sons, and I feel he's safe as a baby here in Chicago. Only suddenly a problem's come up. As you've no doubt heard, the agency's opening a new branch in San Francisco. The chief's planning to go out there to officiate at the opening. They'll be preparing to roll out the red carpet for him; it's important that he show; it's vital. The papers'll be giving it big coverage. He's dead set on going, of course. He brushes off these threats like so much lint.''

"If he doesn't go it'd blacken the eye that never closes,'' said Doc grinning.

"It's no joke. If the king of the hill doesn't show up . . .''
Raider interrupted, raising his hand like a schoolboy. "Couldn't he let word out to the newspapers that he's too sick to travel? He's sure not a hundred percent.''

Wagner shook his head. "Every paper in the country knows about the letters.''

"How did they find out?'' Raider asked.

"Raider, finding out everything from your Aunt Tillie's age to how much Marshall Field pays his elevator girls is a newspaper's strongest suit. The point is if he doesn't go, they'll lower the boom on him. They'll print cartoons of him hiding behind his wife or under the sofa over there. Besides, the Grand Army of the Republic couldn't keep him here. He leaves day after tomorrow. And you're going along to protect him.''

"Oh boy,'' moaned Raider.

Wagner fish-eyed him. "What's your problem?''

"Nothing. Only protecting him is going to be like protecting a bull with a wasp up it's hind end. He won't do a damn thing we ask him to. He doesn't listen to you, to his sons, his wife—how are we supposed to get him to cooperate? Tie him up and dump him in a mailbag?''

"You're clever, capable. You'll get him around to your way of thinking."

Raider grunted. Doc shook his head slowly.

"I know what we should be doing. Gang up on him and talk him out of going. Cook up a plausible, perfectly legitimate excuse."

Wagner shook his head. "It's been tried. If his own wife can't get through to him, how can you expect any of us to? His mind's made up; he's going."

The door opened. Pinkerton came back in. "Be prepared, boys, oxpect a nice fat gob of mood to be thrown ot us in tomorrow's edition of thot domned scondal sheet of his. I told him politely, boot in no unsairtain terms, thot we don't have room in oor case load for his dispute with Miss Thompson." He snickered. "You should see the welt across his foorehead where she caught him with her whip."

Wagner cleared his throat nervously. "Chief, Weatherbee and Raider here are going along with you to San Francisco."

"Bushwah. Ahhhh, so that's why you've hauled 'em all the way bock from Great Falls—to play nursemaid to the auld mon. Forget it, the three of you. I'm troveling by my lonesome, ond let me tell you why. He who trovels alone is far less conspicuous. A bodyguard is like a flag, it canna' help boot ottroct ottention." He snatched up the letters, crushing them in his fist and flinging them into the wastebasket. "I'll nae be ontimidated by a pock of illiterate mongrels. Of oll the oonmitigated gall; did you notice? They spelled my name with boot one 'l.' "

He stared from one to the next, his eyes softening. "See here, lods, I oppreciate your concern for my welfare, boot this isn't the first time I've sauntered onder the sword of Domocles. Ond it won't be the lost. I've been shot ot more times thon I con remember; I've gotten a hoondred threatening letters, I've fought my way oot of corners with my bare knuckles, ond I've survived ond thrived. Make nae mistake, I'm nae going into this thing oonprepared.

"Will, what do you think of this for a bright idea? I plon to disguise myself in the vestments of a mon of the cloth, on

Episcopal priest, I think, black on black on black, hard collar and oll. I foncy I might even corry a prayer book in plain sight. A sootle touch, nae? I olso ontend to dye my hair ond beard gray os a fish. 'Twill lend me a dostinguished look, don't you think?''

"Sounds clever," said Doc blandly.

"Clever? It's inspired!" He placed a fatherly hand on Doc's shoulder, then Raider's. "So you see, lods, on this trip I've no need for your boon coomponionship or services, capable though they be. You know the auld saying, he trovels best who trovels alone.''

"Fastest," murmured Doc.

"Eh?''

"Nothing, sir."

"Well, it's been a bonny pleasure seeing you both again. Will here will orrange for your return posses. Keep up the good work oot there. Good-bye for noo, wish me good journey, ond don't forget your soddle, Raider. One o' the ladies might trip over it ond break a leg.''

They left, feeling hustled out verbally if not physically. They started down the hall. They were passing the landing on their way down to the street door when Wagner came hurrying down after them.

"Hold it, stay where you are," he blurted. "Pay no attention to him.''

"Of course not," said Doc, "he's only the boss."

"He only signs our paychecks and pushes our pins all over the territories," added Raider. "Only next time would you mind talking it over with him first before you drag us all the way back here?''

"Listen to me! *You're* going to San Francisco."

"*He* is," said Raider airily. "*We're* heading back to Great Falls." He shifted his saddle to the other shoulder, narrowly missing the superintendant's head as he did so and mumbling an apology.

"Listen," rasped the older man, his tone verging on desperation. "If *he's* going to be traveling in disguise, why can't you two?''

Doc sighed. "As what, Tom Thumb and Jumbo the elephant?"

"As . . . as whatever you like. You decide."

"It wouldn't work," said Raider. "We'd have to be in the same car with him. We'd have to stick to him like shoe leather. The man's got an eye like a red-tailed hawk. He'd spot us two minutes after the train pulled out."

"Not if you split up. You can take turns watching him. Think about it. Don't be so negative. There's a few things in our favor. For one, nobody's going to try anything while the train's moving. What they'll probably do is cook up some sort of diversion."

"How do you know anybody's even gunning for him?" asked Doc. "You know as well as we do, nine out of ten threatening letters are, to use his favorite word, bushwah."

"Not these. This bunch is out to get him." Wagner nodded once, punctuating this assertion.

Raider began running down possible ways of doing so, thinking out loud. "They could derail the train, stage a holdup."

Wagner nodded. "Take advantage of a scheduled stop, a stop for fuel or water. The simplest and least noticeable way of all would be to get him in his berth while he and everybody else is asleep. That's where you two come in. You guard the doors at both ends so nobody gets in or out."

"Getting back to my original question," said Doc, "what would we use for disguises?"

"Disguises be damned," grumbled Raider. "If you stop talking long enough to think about it, none of it makes a damn lick o' sense. You're asking us to protect a man who's already turned thumbs down on the idea. Made up his mind he can take care of himself. He doesn't need us, doesn't want us, and if he finds out he's got us he'll hit the ceiling. Likely have us tossed off into a gully full o' gravel." He paused and brightened. "I got an idea. Why not ship him to Frisco in a damn hot-air balloon?"

Wagner curled his lip slightly in disdain, but otherwise bridled his reaction.

"We can stand here jawing and making jokes all day," he

said tightly, worry creasing his ample brow. "But what it boils down to is plain: The man's got to be protected. Even, as it appears, against himself, his damned cock-sureness. And you two are elected. We've less than forty-eight hours to get up something like a workable strategy. I want you to drop by the office after work this evening. I'll have a copy of his itinerary for you—his car, his berth number, everything you'll need to know. Oh, and one other thing . . ."

"Not something that might help," said Doc.

"A possible complication. It seems that the Adams Express Company is sending a couple hundred thousand cash out to the U.P. office in Ogden on the same train. Adams, as you know, is one of our biggest accounts. We're assigning three operatives to the baggage car. See that you two stay clear of it. Regardless of what may happen. You've one assignment only: Protect the chief. Get him to San Francisco, keep an eye on him while he's there, and get him back here in one piece."

Footsteps sounded, descending from above. "Somebody's coming. I've got to get back up. He's going to be wondering where I've gotten to. He generally leaves the office at five on the dot; I want you two back here at five-fifteen. We'll put our heads together and iron out the rough spots." He glanced at his watch. "You've got roughly five hours to get hold of disguises. Needless to say, they'd better be good. They'd better be perfect. I'll see you at five-fifteen sharp." He paused. "And Raider . . ."

"Yeah?"

"Store that saddle in supply before you crown somebody. And your spurs. You won't be needing either to ride a train."

CHAPTER TWO

Doc considered his idea for their disguises brilliant; Wagner approved of it wholeheartedly; only Raider had misgivings. Doc's plan was for the two of them to exchange appearances. Doc would dress like Raider, from disreputable-looking Stetson down to jangling daisy rowel spurs, affecting a slightly bow-legged saunter and day-old beard. Raider would dress, as he put it, like a damn window dummy, in a tailored cheviot suit, cardsharper's silk vest, overgaiters, button shoes in place of boots, and hard-boiled hat.

"You got me looking like a damn riverboat squaredecker!"

"Just keep your mouth shut," advised his partner. "Stick to nodding and smiling, and, oh yes, get yourself a tooth-brush and some Amberson's Floral Mint Mouthwash."

"You go to hell!"

The three had reconvened in Wagner's office after working hours as planned, and Raider and Doc were given all the necessary information regarding the chief's itinerary. According to Wagner, A.P. was sticking by his guns, traveling disguised as a clergyman. His train was scheduled to leave Union Station for Omaha at twelve noon sharp. Once arrived in Omaha he would transfer to the Union Pacific transcontinental, which would take him to Ogden, Utah, where he would change over to the Central Pacific for the final run to Oakland and the ferry to San Francisco.

Traveling westward with him would be the Adams Express money shipment under the watchful eyes of three Pinkerton operatives.

Jayhawker Justice had issued no further death threats. Final plans were made for the chief's departure two days hence. Raider and Doc were to be boarding the train in the yards as soon as it was made up. When it puffed its way into the station, Pinkerton would board, following his farewells to his wife Joan, son William, and Wagner.

Unfortunately, Wagner's carefully devised plan for sneaking Raider and Doc on board ran into complications. When the superintendent came down to the station to see the chief off on the noon train, he, Wagner, found William Pinkerton all by himself, waiting for him. To Wagner's chagrin he was told that William's father had taken an earlier train and was already fifty minutes on his way. Meanwhile, his two artfully disguised would-be bodyguards were settling comfortably into their seats at opposite ends of a passenger car in the yards, waiting for the noon train to move out to the boarding platform. Wagner hurried to the yards, found Raider and Doc, and told them what had happened.

Hiring horses, they chased the Omaha-bound train, catching up with it just outside Rock Island near the Illinois border, where it had stopped to take on water. The two were preparing to board when Raider chanced to look up the way at the very moment two men were getting off the first car. Wedged between them, ostensibly in their custody, was a burly-looking man of medium height dressed entirely in black and displaying a gray beard.

"Doc!" bellowed Raider pointing.

Doc let go of the boarding rails and dropped back down. Pushing Raider ahead of him, they began running alongside the train. The whistle hooted, the driving wheels spun, the stack belched smoke, cinders shot upward and came showering down, and the three men who had disembarked got into a waiting democrat wagon and drove away in the direction of Moline. Off chugged and rumbled the train as Raider and Doc raced back to their well-lathered horses, which were being held by a boy who had promised—for two dollars cash—to take them to the nearest livery stable.

From there Wagner was to be contacted to send a man out to retrieve them.

Mounting up, the two Pinkertons gave chase to the fast-moving wagon. They caught up with it less than a mile from the tracks, coming up on either side, waving their guns and ordering the driver to rein up.

He did so, glowering.

"Who in hell are you two?" he sputtered.

"What do you think you're doing?" queried his companion, his hands upraised.

Doc flashed his I.D. "We're Pinkertons. You just took this man off the train. Forcibly. We were watching. He . . ." He paused, swallowed, and turned his eyes slowly toward Raider, who was on the other side of the wagon.

"It's not him," murmured Raider, mystified.

The man in black seated between his two abductors, staring at Raider and Doc from behind his gray beard, wore no clerical collar. Close up, he bore not the slightest resemblance to Allan Pinkerton. His face was thinner, his eyes darker, and he looked to be at least ten years younger than the chief. Doc lowered his weapon; Raider did likewise; the two men they had accosted lowered their arms.

"Pinkertons or no, you two better goddamn explain yourselves!" exclaimed the driver.

"We were boarding the train," said Doc. "From down the tail end where we were getting on this fellow looked like him."

"Like who?"

"The chief, Allan Pinkerton."

Raider nodded, his eyes downcast.

"We got news for you," said the driver, his tone sneering. "This boy happens to be Joseph Edward Durant, wanted for conspiracy to defraud the U.S. government. The details is none o' your business." He waved a paper at Doc. "This here's a warrant for his arrest. You want to look it over, or you want to take the word o' the Secret Service, which my friend here and I happen to be working for?"

"I'll take your word for it."

"That's mighty generous of you, neighbor."

"Speak up, Joe," said his partner. "Tell him you're not Allan Pinkerton."

"We apologize for delaying you," said Doc sheepishly.

The driver laughed. "Looks to me like you're the ones delayed." He waggled a finger down the tracks. The train had all but vanished from sight. "Hang around if you like. There's another train through Rock Island in four hours. Git-up!"

Slapping the mares' rumps sharply, he started the wagon lurching forward. Off they drove, all three occupants laughing. Doc stared at Raider standing opposite him.

"Rade, I think it's high time you got your eyes examined."

"Me? What about you?"

As matters stood at the moment it was not a particularly encouraging state of affairs. Here was Allan Pinkerton riding the rails to Omaha, comfortable in the confidence that his clerical garb was all the protection he needed to throw his would-be assassins off his trail. Here were Raider and Doc, each of them uncomfortably masquerading as the other, despite the obvious differences in their heights and builds, marooned on the discouragingly desolate border separating Illinois and Iowa, watching the Omaha train carrying Allan Pinkerton dissolve into the cloudless blue sky edging the horizon. As Doc perused the three-page history of the Clancys given him by William Wagner, Raider silently reread the third and most recent Jayhawker Justice letter threatening Allan Pinkerton with death.

"I got a hunch, Doc," said Raider, looking up from the letter. "I'll bet you a new Winchester against four sour apples these Jayhawker bastards are just blowing off steam."

"Wishful thinking, Rade," said Doc, without looking up from his own reading.

"Think about it. Killing A.P. isn't going to help them six snakes in the pen in Lincoln. Not a lick. But kidnapping could. They could hold him hostage, tell the governor to let the Clancys go, or else—"

"Read them again, Rade. You'll see they're talking killing, not kidnapping."

"I know what they're talking. I still say it's a bluff. The smartest thing they can do would be to grab him, cache him away somewheres, contact Governor Whoozis—"

"Garber."

"—and pressure him into letting the Clancys walk. He's got the authority, and he's got a great excuse to. He doesn't want to endanger the life o' the Great Law Enforcer. At worst he could downgrade their sentences to life. That way they'd have a chance."

"For what?"

"For lots o' things: a new trial, parole, to break out. . . . When you're alive anything can happen; when you're dead the game's over."

Doc rubbed his chin thoughtfully. "I don't know. If they're planning on kidnapping him, why wouldn't they say so?"

"Why give it away? Lay on the big threat, that's the best play. And if they get hold o' him and send out word they got him, with his watch or something to prove it, you can bet your buckle Garber'll think twice about going through with the hangings."

"That's all conjecture, Rade, nothing but. How can you say what's in someone else's mind in this kind of situation? Let's get out of here. We can talk and ride at the same time."

"Not on these two hay bales. They're 'bout ready for the boneyard. Get out the map and let's have a look."

Doc fumbled in his bag and brought out a sheaf of maps, selecting one covering the area.

"How far do you figure to Omaha?" asked Raider.

"Six or seven hours by train. By horse, don't ask. Rade?"

"Yeah?"

"I'm getting a crazy idea. Wild. Downright devious."

"What?"

"Think about it—there's no way now we're going to catch up with that train, right? Certainly not before it gets to Omaha. But what if we could arrange it so that's as far as it gets? As far as *he* gets."

"How?"

"Let's go on to Rock Island. We've got to contact Wagner. It's past five; he'll probably be on his way home. Burnside, the night man, can get a message to him."

"What message? What are you talking about?"

"Let's go."

A demonic grin spread over Doc's handsome face. Raider had seen that look before, he recalled, a chill, worrisome feeling settling in his stomach as he recognized it.

Doc's plan to delay Allan Pinkerton in Omaha until they could catch up with him was more than devious; it was, by his own admission, malicious, even stone-hearted. Before emigrating to America from Glasgow in 1842 Pinkerton had met and married Joan Carfrae. She had been a bookbinder's apprentice from Paisley just outside Glasgow and had sung with the Unitarian choir. The two fell deeply in love. Pinkerton proposed, was accepted, and off they sailed to America, eventually settling outside Chicago. To earn a living Pinkerton turned his hand to the one trade he had experience in, coopering. Leaving his Joan in Chicago, he journeyed to nearby Dundee and went to work making barrels, churns, and tubs. He worked long and hard, saved his money, and in time built a small house in Dundee attached to a work shed that bore a sign reading ALLAN PINKERTON, COOPERAGE. By 1847, five years after landing in the new world, Pinkerton's business was flourishing. He now employed eight full-time workers. He might have continued as a cooper the rest of his life, but in looking for wood in the area surrounding his workshop, he chanced upon the meeting place of a band of counterfeiters on a small island in the neighborhood. Hiding in the tall grass on shore, he watched the gang at work one night and the next day notified the local sheriff. Sheriff Dearborn and Pinkerton headed a posse, raided the island hideout, arrested the counterfeiters, and confiscated their bogus coins and tools.

Pinkerton's reputation as a "detective" quickly spread, and other assignments came to him. Counterfeiting was the crime of the times, and nine out of every ten cases he took on had to do with tracking down and getting the goods on the duplicators of everything from dimes to fifty-dollar bills. In nearby burgeoning Chicago, meanwhile, where his beloved Joan sat patiently awaiting his summons, outlaws of every description were active. Back to Chicago came Mr. and Mrs. Pinkerton, and in 1849 newly elected Mayor Boone appointed the young Scot as the city's first authorized detective. Despite the risks and uncertainties of Allan's new calling, Joan staunchly supported him. To his associates—and later to their two sons and daughter—he described her as a woman of great courage and enormous devotion to him. He might also have added that she was a woman of infinite patience; along with raising her children almost single-handedly, she concealed and fed literally hundreds of runaway slaves, sharing her husband's tireless efforts in the abolitionists' cause before and during the recent Civil War.

Doc's idea, his fire with which they would fight the fire of Allan Pinkerton's obstinacy, was to be Mrs. Allan Pinkerton.

CHAPTER THREE

When the train, carrying among its passengers the Reverend Dr. Walter Strawson of the Michigan Avenue Episcopal Church of Chicago, reached Omaha, Strawson took advantage of the announced twenty-minute layover to step off the train and stretch his legs. No sooner had he reached the platform than his hearing was abused by a shrill voice calling his assumed name.

"Telegram for Reverend Strawson. Telegram for Reverend Strawson."

"Here, son."

Pinkerton signed his alias, handed the boy a nickel, and began reading the message. Its contents all but stopped his heart, widening his eyes in astonishment. The information responsible for his reaction of alarm had been deliberately couched in vague terms, but the gist of it was that a domestic dilemma of great magnitude had erupted and it was absolutely vital that he remain in Omaha until further explanation arrived. The initial at the bottom, J, patently announced that the sender could be no one else but Mrs. Pinkerton.

"What the hell is going on?" he blurted, attracting a questioning and critical glance from a fetching young lady passing by him, twirling her parasol. Such language in such a tone from one wearing a clerical collar clearly disturbed her.

The train left on schedule, minus one passenger in addition to those who had planned to get off in Omaha. Pinkerton loitered about the Western Union office for two hours, pacing and fuming and repeatedly questioning the clerk, asking if any message had come in for Reverend Strawson. The Union

Pacific transcontinental, which he had planned to change to, came and went without him. No further word from Joan was forthcoming. He sent off six wires, two to his wife, four to Wagner at his home, asking, requesting, finally demanding to know what was going on. He got no responses. He got increasingly impatient, muttering and grumbling to himself, his face reddening to the color of an October beet. At length he became furious, abandoning completely the placid demeanor customarily associated with men of the cloth.

A train finally arrived at seven minutes before nine in the evening. The sight of it cooled his choler, and when the conductor told him that they would be traveling all the way to Ogden, the semblance of a joyous twinkle crept into his eyes. Nevertheless, he continued deeply worried over the wire from his wife, and he couldn't understand why neither she nor Wagner had answered him.

Boarding the train and walking down the aisle to the seat assigned him, he steadied himself, casually glancing at his fellow passengers in passing. His eye fell on a well-dressed gentleman occupying a window seat. Extraordinarily well dressed, impeccably so, but somehow, insisted the chief's instincts, out of character in such an ensemble. To Pinkerton's experienced eye the fellow looked more like a cowhand than a fashion plate, his slouch, the toothpick dangling from the corner of his mouth, his deeply tanned and weathered complexion—evidence of a life spent mostly out of doors—his gnarled and rawboned hands were none of the characteristics generally distinguishing a flawlessly tailored urbanite.

What followed as Pinkerton passed the man confirmed his suspicions. Evidently recognizing the Reverend Strawson from his reflection in the window, the man sitting was unable to resist turning to look at him. Their eyes met. Pinkerton gasped.

"Shit!" muttered Raider.

"*Raider!*" bellowed the chief, startling the entire car.

"Ah . . . ah . . ." Raider grimaced, swallowed, and tried a bluff. "Sorry, stranger, you got me mixed up with somebody else. The name is . . . is . . ."

It suddenly struck him that he had neglected to take on a phony name to match his disguise.

"Raider, you horse's—"

An elderly matron sitting behind Raider gasped, cutting Pinkerton off in mid-sentence. He sat down alongside Raider.

"What the hell are you doing here?" He clenched his teeth, seething, instantaneously livid. "I gave you strict orders not to follow me! Strict ond irrevorsible. I've a mind to fire you on the spot. By oll that's holy thot's exoctly what I'll do. You dare disobey your sooperior, Will Wogner . . ."

"We did like he . . . We did not, no sir!"

"What do you mean 'we'?" Understanding inundated Pinkerton's fired eyes. "Ah-hah! So Weatherbee's here too, is he?"

"He's up front." Raider indicated. "First seat on the left. Chief, I'll tell you the God's honest truth, this wasn't our idea at all. Wagner asked us, ordered us to keep an eye on you. Which, if you please just think about it, makes sense. It does. He assigned us to go along for the ride. Not get in your way. Not even talk to you. Handle it so you wouldn't even know we're around. Just in case somebody tries something. You can't go blaming him, or your missus."

Understanding arrived a second time. "Ah-hah! You missed the train in Chicago, of coorse, what with me lighting oot early. You couldn't cotch oop with me so you sent thot phony wire to delay me so I'd miss the earlier troncontinental. To give you the time you needed to cotch oop—ond even hod the goll to sign Mrs. Pinkerton's name to your nonsensicol drivel."

"We did like hell! Wagner did, and with her okay. For Chrissakes, can't you get it through your head? Everybody's worrying about you, her most of all. Everybody except you, you pig-headed—"

"*Enoof!* On your feet."

"What for? Where we going?"

"Up front between the cars. Where you ond me ond thot tinhorn partner of yours con talk in a wee bit o' privacy. *March*!"

• • •

The Sight of Doc Weatherbee done up like a smaller version of Raider, side by side with Raider done up like an oversized Weatherbee, appeared so ridiculous to Pinkerton it could not help but soften his rancor against the two. One look in the privacy of the vestibule obliged him to cover his mouth with his hand to keep from laughing uproariously. But as comical as they looked, seeing them impressed upon him the realities of his situation heretofore blocked out of mind by his conceit and his well-known tendency to turn conveniently deaf when others offered sound advice.

So he capitulated, though about as graciously as any practicing power inflated dictator.

"Since you've made it this far with your duplicity ond flagront disregard for orders, you might joost as well stay on for the ride. But there's a few things I feel coompelled to set you straight on. The first thing you'll do is get oot of those preposteroos getups ond into proper clothing. You, Raider, look like you should be stonding in one of those pansy men's shop windows with a wood rod jommed oop your bockside, ond you, Weatherbee, look like a domned condy butcher working a Wild West show. Have either of you ever seriously coonsidered voodville?"

"Chief," said Doc, ignoring the barb, "we've worked out a plan to protect you that we both think makes sense."

"Have you noo? Isn't thot grond."

"Your berth is located in the first car after the tender. It's actually a parlor car, but it's been converted to make room for four berths. One of us will be sleeping in there under or over you, whichever you prefer. The other'll stand guard at the door at this end."

"What aboot the door thot opens on the tender?"

"That'll be locked from the time you go to bed to when you get up in the morning."

"Thot makes sense. I'll speak to the trainmon myself."

Doc shook his head. "Better one of us talk to him. As far as any of the personnel or passengers know, you're Reverend Strawson. Why let anybody know Allan Pinkerton is a passenger? What good will your disguise do you then?"

"Oll right, oll right, hondle it os you see fit."

"During the day, every time we stop, for whatever reason," went on Doc, "we'll be close by, one of us in front of you, the other covering your back."

"We've got four days travel ahead of us," said Raider. "From Omaha to Ogden, change over to the Central Pacific, and on to Frisco."

Doc nodded. "One other thing. I'll get hold of a copy of the passenger manifest from the conductor."

"Why would he give it to you?" asked Pinkerton.

Doc showed his I.D. card. "The agency's still working for the Union Pacific. I'll get it, and there'll be no need to explain why I want it."

"He'll guess I'm the reason. He moost read the noosepapers. Besides, I con't see as a list of the possengers will help you ony. Onybody olready on board or getting on oop ahead looking for me won't be likely to give his real name."

"That's true. Still, I'd like a copy of that list."

Looking down the length of the train through the succession of door windows, they could see passengers making their way to the sleeping cars in the middle of the train.

"Here coom the sheep home to the fold," observed the chief. He yawned. "I'm aboot ready to turn in myself."

"Doc," said Raider, "get on up front and get that forward door locked, okay?"

Pinkerton nodded. "Check ond see hoo many keys there are to the door ond who hos 'em."

"I'll cover the door at this end," continued Raider. "Once you lock up, get yourself some sleep. You can spell me around two o'clock." He cast a look inside the empty parlor car and the four-berth compartment beyond the plush chairs at the far end. Then he glanced back at Doc.

His partner's expression was suddenly grim.

"What's the motter?" asked Pinkerton.

"It just occurred to me," said Doc. "We know which car you'll be in; we can lock the door at the other end and guard the door at this end, but how are we going to know if whoever's after you isn't going to be occupying one of the two other berths in there? He could be under you, over you, across from you . . .''

Pinkerton laughed dryly. ''We'll oll three cross our fingers ond pray they're both reserved for two loovely ladies.'' Once more he yawned. ''Hoppy dreams, lods.''

CHAPTER FOUR

The night passed without incident, the first of the four required to close the distance between Omaha and the West Coast. Most of the following day, between meals taken in the dining car with the other passengers, was spent in the Victorian elegance of the parlor portion of the car hooked to the tender. To the three Pinkertons' surprise and satisfaction the discovery was made that the door leading to the tender was so constructed that it could be barred inside, making it unnecessary to lock it from the outside.

One of the four compartment berths was not in use, the passenger for whom it had been reserved having canceled his trip shortly before the train departed Omaha. Allan Pinkerton chose one of the two upper berths, and Doc and Raider took turns sleeping in the berth below the chief's. The lower berth across from theirs was occupied by the Honorable Thaddeus Wollaston, a senator from California. He was on his way home to San Francisco following the end of the latest session of Congress in Washington.

The senator was a garrulous sort whose favorite pastimes appeared to be chain-smoking odoriferous panatellas, enabling him to discharge clouds of smoke very nearly rivaling in quantity those issuing from the locomotive's stack, and downing tumblers of Cuban rum which caused him to sweat like a Nueces steer, but curiously failed to thicken his speech, blear his eyes, or otherwise induce him to abandon sobriety. Raider offered an explanation for this: "The man sweats it out so fast it doesn't have time to boil his brain. He's probably never been pie-eyed in his life. What a gift," he marveled, his whisper steeped with envy and unheard by the senator. "Imagine drinking your guts full and never feeling a thing."

Pinkerton was not impressed. He himself was a lifelong teetotaler, and the drinking prowess of others, as prodigious as their capacities might be, failed to arouse his admiration. His only comment was that two-fisted drinkers had no business holding high public office, which prompted Raider to rejoin that if politicians were denied liquor, their numbers in Congress would probably be reduced by 98 percent.

His puffing and guzzling notwithstanding, Senator Wollaston proved an interesting traveling companion. His memory was stocked with amusing stories, most of them sufficiently off-color to redden the chief's cheeks under his whiskers. Wollaston also divulged all the latest Washington gossip. Loose and tireless though his tongue may have been, he admitted to holding the Reverend Strawson's collar and his calling in the highest esteem.

"My mother wanted me to enter the ministry. The Lord and the Devil wrestled over me for quite some time." He raised his glass, downing a swig. "It's plain to see who won. Just the same, saving souls, steering the wanderer back onto the path of righteousness, has to be immensely gratifying."

Pinkerton grunted and forced a friendly smile. Wollaston turned to Raider and Doc.

"And what do you two do for a living?" He stared at Raider. "You in beef cattle?"

"On and off."

"How about you?" Wollaston asked Doc.

"I sell gentlemen's footwear. Perhaps you've heard of our company—Selz Liberty Bell Shoes?"

"Can't say that I have. Are you sure you three wouldn't like a cigar or a snort?"

Raider licked his lips and glanced at Pinkerton. The expression he got in response quelled any hope he might have had of accepting the senator's offer. Doc also declined.

"I'm curious," said the senator, lighting up a fresh cigar fully eight inches long and as green as a lily pad. "You three seem unlikely traveling companions; a sky pilot, a shoe drummer, and a cowboy.''

"We met joost before we boarded in Omaha ond found we'd all three been given reservations in this porticular cor,'' said Pinkerton.

"You two''—Wollaston aimed his cigar first at Raider, then Doc—"only slept half the night last night. You, cowboy, came in at two, and you, Mr. Selz Liberty Bell Shoes, got up, got dressed, and left. I've been thinking about that. It's like the two of you were guarding the Reverend Dr. Strawson here. Four hours on, four off.''

"Guarding him?'' asked Raider, feigning astonishment. "Why would we do that? Why would he need guarding?''

Wollaston chuckled, winked, and, thrusting his hand under his seat cushion, brought out a copy of the Omaha *World-Herald*. He read aloud:

" 'Pinkerton National Detective Agency to Open New Office in San Francisco.' Ahem. 'Mr. Allan Pinkerton, founder and chief of the world-famous Pinkerton Detective Agency, has been invited to San Francisco to preside over ceremonies celebrating the opening of the agency's newest office. Mr. Pinkerton will be traveling to the Coast by transcontinental railroad. His journey from Chicago is particularly noteworthy in light of the recent threats against his person previously reported by this newspaper. Three letters have been received by Chief Pinkerton addressed to the agency's Chicago office. A facsimile of the latest threat can be found on page four.' ''

"Coongrotulations, Senator Wollaston, if indeed thot's your true name ond title,'' said Pinkerton evenly. "You're a most persoptive individual.''

"Not very. Let's say I'm just not stupid.'' Wollaston sighed. "Dear me. I do wish I could say your secret is safe with me, only seeing as it's in practically every newspaper in North America it doesn't appear to be a secret to anybody, unless one's deaf, dumb, and blind. I confess I don't know the first thing about criminology, the techniques, the tricks of the trade, but in the face of this . . .'' He tapped the paper and the photograph of Allan Pinkerton as Allan Pinkerton.

"How in God's name do you expect to get to Frisco and back without being cut down in a hail of bullets?" A look of genuine concern came into his rum-reddened eyes. "There could be fifteen assassins on board at this very minute, possibly drawing straws to pick the one who's to do the deed."

"That's our worry, Senator," said Raider quietly.

Pinkerton nodded. "Exoctly."

"But what about me? I don't fancy getting caught in the middle of a shoot-out. I've got a wife and seven children, and a lady friend in Sacramento. Suddenly, through no doing of my own, here I am in the middle of a private war." He emptied his glass in one gulp. "I don't like it, boys, not a bit. I'm not the stuff that heroes are made of. I think you'd better change trains, or I'd better. Somebody better. The shooting's liable to start any minute."

"My friend," said Pinkerton, "take a wee whit of advice from an auld hond. Don't ponic. You'll nae be caught in ony shoot-oot."

"Nobody's gunnin' for you," remarked Raider.

"You don't understand, damn it! I could easily be the innocent victim of this . . . this vendetta of yours. You think that collar and that beard and hair are going to fool these Jayhawker scum?"

The conversation grew more and more heated. Finally, the chief proposed a solution. Senator Wollaston would put in for a change of accommodations. The porter would move him bag and baggage, cigars and rum, five cars down the train to the last sleeper. He would henceforth take his meals in the sleeping car, and until the train arrived in Ogden there would be no need whatsoever for him to set foot out of the car.

"To be brootily fronk, gontlemen," confided the chief to Raider and Doc, "locking the fat sot oop, cutting him ond his big mouth off from the other possengers, is the smartest move we con make. The way this trovesty seems to be going it's the only move."

CHAPTER FIVE

The transcontinental raced across the Nebraska prairie bound for Cheyenne, the first-class passengers wining and dining on pheasant, stuffed quail, sweetbreads potted and smothered with mushrooms, baked rabbit pie, croquettes of oysters, chicory and lobster salad, and dozens of other delicacies familiar to the palates of princes and potentates, twelve courses in all and forty-five dishes to choose from for dinner alone. The sumptuous bill of fare to some extent distracted the travelers from thoughts of train robbers; derailments caused by Indians angered by the iron horse's invasion of their hunting grounds; enormous herds of buffalo assembling on the tracks, creating an obstacle of beef and bone half a mile thick; and that most frightening threat of all, the prairie fire, ignited by sparks from the smokestack, lightning, or Indians' torches, and capable of laying waste hundreds of square miles. The prairie fire and its dreaded consequences made for many a lurid tale, including one recounted by Allan Pinkerton at dinner one evening. He told his wide-eyed listeners of a train pulling eleven wooden coaches that tried to run through a fire before the flames on either side reached the tracks.

"Oonfortunately, the winds coom up strong of a sudden ond oll oleven cars caught fire ond were reduced to oshes in minutes, cooking the oocuponts like herring in a tin."

But there were pleasanter sights in crossing Nebraska than train robbers, on-charging Indians, or prairie fires. Wild fowl winged through the azure skies. Blacktail deer, antelope, and elk cavorted about the landscape, the weather was pleasant, and the train rolled on at a steady pace.

29

Senator Thaddeus Wollaston appeared to be the only passenger on board who had penetrated Allan Pinkerton's disguise. But, observed Doc confidently, the senator would keep his discovery to himself. No one knew better than he that his silence was his safest protection.

None of the other passengers showed the slightest curiosity in the Reverend Dr. Walter Strawson. Evidently, few found the time to read the Omaha *World-Herald* or any other newspaper, so absorbing was the scenery, so enjoyable the meals.

The train crossed the border into Wyoming Territory. Beyond Cheyenne the tracks ran up close to the foothills of the Laramie Range and then curved around them. In the distance rose the northern Rockies, not nearly as lofty as the southern spine of the chain, shadowing eastern Colorado, but like it laced with chasms, ravines, and tumbling streams, pierced with tunnels hewn from solid rock, and mantled with dense green growth.

The time was shortly after ten o'clock at night. The moon overhead was full, flat, and as cold-looking as a ball of ice. Twinkling stars crowded about it. Raider was sprawled out in the parlor car, his boots off, his bloodshot eyes staring aimlessly out at the night. He battled the temptation to close them, and listened to the chief's muffled snoring behind the closed berth compartment door. Suddenly he heard the banshee-screeching sound of wheels braking. The engine struck something in its path. Raider was hurled from his chair. He landed sprawling on hands and knees, coming within an inch of hammering the compartment door with the top of his head. Lurching to his feet, he instinctively grabbed for his gun. The floor angled slightly beneath his feet. Whatever the engine had hit had jolted the train its full length, as if giant hands had grasped the smoke box of the locomotive and the last car vestibule, squeezing them like an accordion. Inside the compartment the impact had thrown Doc and the chief forward in their berths, their bodies jackknifing and tumbling to the floor. Doc landed on top of Pinkerton and the chief bellowed. Raider jerked open the compartment door.

"You two okay?"

"Okay," muttered Doc.

"Speak for yourself, Weatherbee," growled the chief.

Turning, Raider approached the door opening onto the vestibule. Doc and Pinkerton followed. Raider pulled open the door. Down through the cars consternation reigned, women screaming, men shouting angrily. It was a miracle that the train hadn't toppled over, but apparently the abrupt compressing action on impact had only dislodged the wheels from the rails. Trainmen swinging lanterns were running alongside the train on both sides. It was quickly ascertained that only the engine's driving wheels and its front and rear trucks were still in contact with the tracks. Evidently the engine had hit, its cab end bouncing upward, coming down, and magically settling back onto the rails.

But from the tender on back every car was derailed. A fallen tree proved the culprit. Probably struck by lightning, it had fallen across the tracks.

The passengers were calmed. A message was telegraphed thirteen miles back to Cheyenne, and the announcement was made that a work train was being sent out. No one was in any danger; everyone was instructed to remain on board; anyone getting off would risk encountering wild animals, and the conductor took pains to point out that the Union Pacific could not be held responsible for injuries such as bear maulings, attacks by small and possibly rabid animals, or snakebite. The passengers were assured that the train was in no danger of tipping over. Two doctors on board set about attending to cuts, bruises, and sprains.

"Coffee and doughnuts will be served in the dining car in five minutes," announced the trainman. "Again, everyone is requested to stay on board the train."

The chief sat in his nightshirt and robe, rubbing his forehead and glaring at Doc, silently upbraiding him for landing on top of him. Doc ignored him; he was too busy massaging his shoulder, which had struck Pinkerton in the head. Raider glanced from one to the other and smiled inwardly. He sat with his gun in his lap.

"Will you put thot thing oway?" muttered the chief.

Raider holstered his gun. The end door opened. A round-faced, portly man with grease on his neck and one cheek that looked as if someone had dipped their fingers into a can of it and wiped it on him stuck his head in. He wore a striped-denim work cap and overalls, a red bandanna around his neck, and carried a Handlan lamp with a yellow lens.

"Anybody hurt in here?" he asked.

"Not so's you'd know it," said Raider.

"Glad to hear it. Sorry 'bout the inconvenience. Going to have to ask you to move back to the car behind. The work train's just got here. Boys got to get us back on the rails."

"How bod is the domage?" asked Pinkerton.

"Not much. Pilot's pretty banged up."

"Pilot?"

"Cowcatcher. The fireman got shook up, but he'll be okay. He's tough as a goat. Far as the damage goes, looks like some o' the links and pins got to be replaced, them that are too bent outta shape to be straightened. Big job is getting the wheels back on."

"Hoo do they do it?" asked Pinkerton.

"Jacks, crowbars, muscle. They're working on the tender now. Whole string shouldn't take more'n three or four hours. That's why you boys got to move back. To lighten the weight o' the car. Anybody else up front in the berths?"

"No," said Raider. "There's just us in here."

"Well, when you hear 'em finish with the tender and move on down to here, you move back, okay?"

They could hear voices outside. There was a heavy jolting sound, followed by a chorus of happy shouting.

"Tender's back on," said the man. "You best move back now, if you don't mind. I got to check up front for damage." He nodded toward the berth compartment.

Pinkerton continued massaging his head where Doc's shoulder had struck it.

"There's nae doomage," he said testily. "Joost the bedding moosed oop."

"I got to check all the cars, anyhow. That's my job."

The three Pinkertons started for the door, the chief pulling his robe cord tightly about his waist. At the door he turned to the trainman.

"Hoo did this hoppen, onyway? Didn't the ongineer hov his headlight on? Weren't ony of thom oop front watching?"

"They all were. Engineer seen the tree. Brake boys up top seen it too, but we're carrying a lotta weight, brother."

"Reverend, if you don't mind."

"Beg pardon. You look just like a regular sort in them nightclothes. We hit on account you can't slow no train down and stop her in a couple hundred feet. This ain't no surrey. I wouldn't complain if I was you. It coulda turned out one jim dandy of a wreck. We could all be playing harps right about now."

"I wos noot coomplaining," said Pinkerton icily.

They left the car and moved into the car behind. Through the window Raider could see the trainman move into the berth compartment. Seconds later he came back out, nodded to them, and climbed down.

It took twenty-two minutes by Doc's watch for the crew to reset both front and rear wheels onto the rails. Raider, Doc, and the chief returned to their car. The passengers in the car behind them crowded back into the third car while the crew set to work on the second.

The night dragged on, and the workers moved farther and farther toward the rear. At half past eleven, the novelty of the incident having worn off as far as the chief was concerned, he and Doc went back to their berths. Doc checked the forward door, making certain that the bar across it was still set securely in its supports on either side.

Shortly before two in the morning the job was finished, the train restored to the rails, the fallen tree removed, and everyone back in his bed. The work train started back to Cheyenne. Two long hoots of the transcontinental's whistle signaled "release brakes and proceed." Sand was piped down from the sandbox on top of the boiler, spraying the tracks. The driving wheels spun, gained traction; and the train started out.

At two o'clock Raider went inside to wake Doc in his

upper berth. Across from him the chief snored lustily in his lower, the curtains tightly drawn.

"Doc," whispered Raider. "Wake up for Chrissakes, it's after two."

Doc mumbled in his sleep, licked his lips, rolled over, and resumed snoring.

"Doc!"

Raider shook him roughly. Doc sat up, rubbing his eyes. "What the . . ."

"What's the matter with you? Dreaming about some floozie?"

Both glanced at the drawn curtains of the lower berth opposite. Pressing his forefinger against his lips, Raider stealthily eased one of the two curtains aside. The chief was lying on his stomach, the left side of his face buried in his pillow. On he snored. Raider let the curtain fall. Unbuckling his hardware, he tossed it on the foot of the lower berth under Doc's. Then he climbed in, shedding his Levi's and shirt.

"Don't go waking me up before six now," he cautioned his partner. "I'm beat. I need these four hours and then some."

"Let me have your gun."

"What's with your Diamondback?"

"I want both."

Raider stared, barely able to distinguish the outline of Doc's head and shoulders in the darkness of the narrow compartment. "What's the matter, Doc, you got a funny feeling about something?"

"Rade, this train was stopped and standing for more than four hours. A half-dozen unfriendlies could have sneaked on. Who knows what might happen between now and sunup?"

"My iron's at the foot o' the bed. Just don't get bored and start playing with it. You'll likely shoot off your big toe. Good night."

The train rolled on, picking up speed and turning sharply north toward Laramie. There it stopped for fuel and water and then started out once more, heading toward and then around the Medicine Bow Range. Swinging westward again, it began moving across the Great Divide basin. The sun rose, the color of goldbloom saxifrage, ascending into a washed-out blue sky. Doc woke Raider at six on the dot. He held his watch, the second hand just passing twelve, before his partner's bleary eyes, which were trying hard to focus.

"Jesus Christ, you don't give a man two seconds extra sleep, do you?"

"It's going to be a beautiful day, Rade. You don't want to miss a minute."

"The hell I don't."

"Up, up!"

"Leave me be, goddamn it!"

"Aren't you hungry? Don't you want breakfast?"

Raider was about to offer additional surly response when the sleeper behind the curtains across the way coughed slightly. They could hear the chief sit up, snuffle deeply, and clear his throat. Doc drew the curtains for him.

"Good morning, Chief. Did you sleep . . ."

He stopped abruptly and gawked. The man sitting up and staring back at him looked like Allan Pinkerton. Almost exactly. Almost. Gray hair and beard, snapping dark eyes, the identical deep indentations descending from the interstices at the wings of his nose, the same age, just past sixty . . .

But he was not Allan Pinkerton.

CHAPTER SIX

Doc brought his .38 Diamondback up slowly, setting the muzzle against the man's chest.

"Where is he?"

Slowly the stranger raised his hands, the suggestion of a smile flickering on his lips, vanishing.

"Long gone, I'm afraid."

Raider was on his feet. He grabbed a fist full of the stranger's nightshirt. "Okay, let's stop dancing round the candle before we start. We're going to ask you questions, you're going to answer them. Straight. Doc, give me your penknife."

"What?"

"Give me it!"

Doc continued holding his gun on the man. Raider opened the penknife.

"Second and last time," he said, "where are they taking him?"

"I swear to God on a stack of Bibles as high as you can pile, I don't know."

"Up a little higher with the gun, Doc. Up against his throat. That's it. Mister, you're going to answer me. I'm not even going to have to ask again. I'm just going to take this little old fingernail blade, cut out your left eye, and make you eat it. Chewed or whole, however you prefer. Then I'm going to do the same with your right eye. And when that's done I'm going to stop fooling around and get cruel."

"Mexico. Don't ask me where exactly, I swear to God in heaven I don't know."

Doc made a scoffing sound. "You just swore you didn't know Mexico."

"May I lower my hand?"

"Sure," said Doc. "And if you try anything I'll kill you, and not with any penknife."

"You won't. Not as long as there's a chance of your finding him."

Doc shook his head. "We're not going to find him, you are. You're going to lead us right up to their doorstep, wherever it is. From Siberia to Patagonia!"

The stranger swallowed and sobered visibly. He had guts, reflected Raider, looking on. The pan was hot over the fire and he'd jumped right into it. No doubt figuring sooner or later he'd get a chance to jump out and get away. Raider bent over, searching under the lower berth. Luggage and saddlebags had been shoved underneath, but there was still room to hide. He pulled out an unfamiliar-looking carpetbag, setting it on the bed and opening it.

"Get dressed, Parson."

The stranger began dressing, putting on dickey and clerical collar and a black suit identical to the one worn by Allan Pinkerton.

Doc sighed. "Rade, we're getting farther and farther away from Cheyenne," he said morosely.

"By now about a hundred and fifty miles."

"We just passed through Fort Fred Steele."

"Which means we'll be coming up on Rawlins. That'll be a stop."

"There's something you two've got to understand up front," said the stranger, bowing his head and snapping on his collar.

"They forced you to do this," said Doc. He shoved his gun into his belt uncharacteristically.

"Exactly. They're holding my wife and baby daughter."

Raider sighed. "Oh geez, Doc, I got tears coming into my eyes."

"I swear—"

"We know. Mister, you do more swearing to God than

any man I ever met.'' Raider's disgust set his lean face in a scowl. ''What's your name? What's your line?''

''I am Chad Bolton, the actor.''

''Never heard of you,'' said Doc. ''Let's have your wallet.''

''My real name is Casimir Boldonsky.''

He flushed slightly as he said it. He produced his wallet. Doc snatched it from him.

''It figures they'd get a play actor for the job,'' said Raider to him.

''The heartless bastards abducted the three of us. My poor wife, my poor beautiful Beth-Anne! She's only eighteen. She's not well. This could kill her. I swear if they so much as harm a hair on her head or little Lisa I'll stalk them to the ends of the earth.''

Doc was going through the contents of the wallet. It was crammed with yellowed newspaper clippings. ''Chad Bolton and Clara Morris Impress in Feuillet's *The Sphinx*.'' ''Chad Bolton Assumes Lead Opposite Ada Dyas in *The Banker's Daughter*.''

''You've got your whole history in here,'' he murmured.

''One man in his time plays many parts,'' responded Bolton. *''As You Like It*—Shakespeare,'' he added, smiling at Raider.

Raider riveted him with a glare.

''Your life history, but no pictures of poor beautiful Beth-Anne or the baby,'' Doc went on. ''A man usually carries a picture of his wife on him. Especially when she's as beautiful as Beth-Anne. And there's no baby picture, either. Only you and your leading ladies.''

''Beth-Anne's picture, yes. I mislaid it, I'm afraid.''

''You lyin' son of a bitch!'' said Raider. ''You're no more married than a cow-town whore!''

''Ah,'' said Doc.''Here's something interesting.'' He glanced at Bolton. ''You were paid a tidy sum for this performance, weren't you?''

''You're mistaken. I never got a red cent! I tell you I was forced.''

''Look at this, Rade. A receipt for $2,500 deposited in the

Miners & Merchants Bank in Denver. Casimir, you put a pretty cheap price tag on your hide, don't you?''

"You won't kill me. You can't. You're lawmen, not killers. And as I said before, you need me." He ran his fingertips down the line of his cheekbone along his beard. "This thing's starting to itch. Mind if I take it off?"

"Leave it alone," snapped Doc. "It's staying on. Permanently. From here on in you're not *playing* Reverend Strawson, you *are* Reverend Strawson."

The whistle sounded a single long, mournful blast.

"We're coming into Rawlins. We'll get off, bag and baggage." Raider nodded, punctuating this assertion.

"Then what?" asked Doc in a defeated tone.

"We catch the first train back to Cheyenne. He said Mexico, didn't he? That's where we head."

"They've already got better than a four-hour head start," said Bolton, smiling. Raider growled and smashed him in the jaw, dropping him to one side, his head striking the upper berth support post so hard it nearly fractured his skull. He cried out in pain.

"Cut it out, Rade," said Doc.

"He asked for it. I don't like your goddamn smile, Casimir. Don't put it on again. Next time I see it I'll bust your face into little pieces!"

Bolton sat rubbing his head, clearly reluctant to look up and meet Raider's eyes with his own.

"That fat, greasy little man opened the door for you when he came in here, didn't he?" said Doc.

Bolton nodded. "I was hiding in the woods. I came in and hid under the berth until you and Pinkerton came back in and went to bed."

"Then what?"

"Once I was sure you were both asleep I gave each of you a sniff of . . .'' He paused and, reaching under the berth, groping about, brought out a small can. He unscrewed the top. "Nitrous oxide. Colorless, odorless. I gave your chief enough to put him out for a couple of hours. And you just enough to make doubly sure you wouldn't wake up when

Sam and I were taking Pinkerton out. Sam's the chap who came in here and opened the door for me. When I was sure that you and Pinkerton were under to stay, I let Sam back in to help me with the old man. He must weigh two hundred pounds.''

"How much they pay this Sam?" asked Raider.

Again the station approach whistle sounded.

"It's not important, Rade. Get dressed. We've got to get off this thing. No breakfast, no nothing. Just off and onto the first one heading back to Cheyenne. Only how we get to Mexico from Cheyenne beats me.''

"If they can do it, so can we," said Raider, hauling on his Levi's and buttoning his shirt. "It can be done. I'm going into the john and wash up. You and your damn nitrous whatever-you-call-it gave me a man-sized headache, you bastard. That's another score you and me got to settle. Hell, I'm going to have to get up a list. Keep an eye on him, Doc. If he tries anything, give him one in the mouth." Raider massaged his knuckles and smirked at Bolton. "It gives you a real good feeling inside.''

"Hurry it up, Rade.''

Raider had to wait his turn to get into the bathroom located at the near end of the car behind them. Once inside, he relieved himself, washed, towled down, and came out—almost bumping into the last person he wanted to see.

"Good morning," said Senator Wollaston expansively. "I haven't seen you boys since halfway across Nebraska." He tilted his head to one side and smiled, lowering his voice to a whisper. "What's going on?''

"What are you talking about?''

Wollaston nodded toward the parlor car. Doc and Bolton could be clearly seen through the windows. They were talking animatedly, Bolton seemed to be trying to explain something.

"That's not Allan Pinkerton," said the senator flatly.

"Shut your . . . I mean, keep your goddamn voice down, will you?" Raider pulled him to one side in front of an empty seat. "It's the Reverend Strawson, and you know it.''

"Like hell it is. I got eyes like a hawk. I know a makeup job when I see one, good as it is. And I must say it's damned good. He may look like your boss, the 'Reverend Strawson,' but he's not. So what's going on?"

"Not a damn thing that's any o' your beeswax." A tall, homely woman came up, stared at them briefly, and turning, went into the bathroom. Raider pulled Wollaston out into the vestibule. The train wheels clacked loudly over the rail spacings under their feet. Raider had to raise his voice to be heard.

"I recollect you telling us about your dear wife and seven children back home in Frisco."

"That's right. Emma, the former Emma Bixby, her father's a close friend of Leland Stanford's. As for the children, the five boys' names are—"

"I don't give two shits what their names are. Just shut up and listen. You also said something about your lady friend in Sacramento. Now, get this, Mr. U.S. Congress, and get it good. We got operatives all over the Coast. All I got to do is send off a telegram and in two hours one of our boys will have your lady friend's name and address and anything else I want to know about her."

"Wait just a minute," said Wollaston seething, coloring, his jowls quivering.

"You wait. You want to philander, that's your business. That fellow standing talking to my sidekick is our business. In other words, what you think you're seeing, you ain't seeing at all. You get my drift?"

"Your secret is safe with me," said Wollaston coldly. "I'm an honorable man. My word is my bond."

"I'm betting it is. And I'm betting Emma and the five boys and the rest o' your brood are never going to hear a whisper about your whore in Sac City. On account any story about Chief Pinkerton's troubles in the papers is going to be small print and cat litter alongside the Wollaston scandal. Got it?"

"Yes."

The train was beginning to slow. The bell clanged, announcing their arrival in Rawlins.

"And thanks," said Raider.

"What for?"

"For your big mouth." He clapped his hand on Wollaston's shoulder. "See you have yourself a nice trip on through to Frisco. And give our best to your wife."

CHAPTER SEVEN

The earliest eastbound train coming through from Rock Springs on the other side of Bitter Creek was not due in Rawlins for four hours. Doc's disappointment was rapidly deteriorating into depression. In his eyes everything was against them, beginning with time and distance. Bolton was clearly pleased at the two operatives' frustration, but was sensible enough not to smile about it. After they had eaten breakfast Doc suggested they while away the two hours remaining before their train came in at the local photographers, getting Bolton's picture taken. The three of them stood at the hitch rack in front of the Rawlins House, taking the warm morning sun, Raider working bits of bacon out of his gums with a toothpick. Bolton's beard continued to itch, and he continued to complain about it; but on it would stay, both operatives assured him.

"He looks enough like the chief made up as Strawson to pass on a wanted dodger or in a newspaper picture," said Doc to Raider. "We can get shots taken and when we get to Denver have copies run off. The Denver office can send them out, spread them all the way down to the Mexican border."

"The hell with that!" said Raider. "When we get to Denver we're going nowhere near the agency office. Use your head, for Chrissakes. You want Billy Pinkerton and his brother and Wagner, the whole crowd, to know he's been snatched?"

"They're going to know when the pictures of the good reverend are distributed," said Doc.

43

"Sooner or later they got to know, but for us better later than soon."

"You do have a problem," interposed Bolton, starting, then quickly suppressing, a chuckle.

"Shut up, Casimir," growled Raider.

A stage rumbled by, kicking up dust, filling the street with it. Doc coughed and waved it away from his breathing space.

Raider frowned. "I suppose we could get pictures taken, but how can we be sure the bastards don't take his disguise off?"

"They'd be stupid to do that. His face is too recognizable. Why run the unnecessary risk of his being spotted? Nobody knows him as Strawson but us."

"And the Honorable Thaddeus Wollaston." Raider grinned. "But he going to be doing the best imitation of a clam you ever did see from here on in." He spit out his toothpick and rubbed his hands together. "Okay, let's get Casimir's picture shot. We're going to want you to smile real pretty for the camera, Cas. And just keep playing along like you did in the restaurant, like we're three old saddle pals."

"I wouldn't worry about me spilling the beans."

"I don't, you son of a bitch, not for two seconds."

"You two must realize you don't stand a chance in a million of finding him. And even if you do, you won't come within a hundred yards of him without getting him killed and your own heads shot off."

"Chance is all part of the job," said Doc, yawning, pretending to boredom with the conversation.

"That and more," said Raider, staring at Bolton. "You don't know a damn thing about Allan Pinkerton, do you?"

"Just what I read in the papers, as they say. He was on his way to San—"

"Shut up and listen. I'm going to tell you something about the man. He's like nobody you'll ever know if you live to be six hundred. He can be bitchier than an unballed biddy. He's got no patience. None. He's sarcastic, he's surly, he's insultin', he's about as much fun as a bedroll fulla scorpions. He's ornery as a stone-deaf mule. He's an unfair, loudmouthed, con-fuckin'-tentious, bullyin' know-it-all.''

''He talks too much,'' said Doc.

''That, too. He's predictable as a rattler. He's ungrateful, demanding, peevish. He's tighter than the knot in the noose on the neck of a three-hundred pound horse thief. He's petty, childish—''

''Cynical, smug, arrogant, patronizing, officious—''

''You're forgetting cheap,'' said Raider. ''He pays his people like he was tappin' his heart for blood. But understand this: He's something else that blots out all the bad, all the things folks can't stand about him. He's a man, capital M. He's got more guts than a Sioux war party. He cares about people nobody else gives a shit about. He worked close as sweat to skin with John Brown and all the other abolitionists. He's been shot at and shit on, jumped and stomped and beat up so many times he's lost count. He come over from Scotland on a sailboat and landed in a rowboat. Sailboat sunk. He wasn't in this country three days 'fore him and his wife was robbed of everything they owned. They had to split up so's he could go out and find work to feed 'em and keep clothes on their backs. It was months before they could get back together.

''He made himself something out of nothing, made himself big, successful, important. He's got a wife, two sons, and a daughter who'd lay down their lives for him, they respect him so. And he's got more devotion in his pinky finger for his family than most men got in their whole bodies for theirs. Even senators from California.''

Bolton's face darkened. The last he did not follow, but he said nothing.

''And,'' Doc went on, ''there isn't a soul who works for him, down to the boy who sweeps the office floor, who doesn't accord him the kind of respect most people reserve for princes of the church. The man literally, single-handedly invented the art of criminal investigation in this country. He wrote the book, chapter and verse. He's past sixty now. Ten years ago he had a stroke that crippled him, paralyzed him, nearly killed him, but he survived. When the whole forest goes down, he'll be the last oak standing. That, mister, is Allan Pinkerton.''

"What it comes down to is this," said Raider. "If the boot was on the other foot, if it was him having to chase down somebody who'd captured us, any Pinkertons, he'd be as hot after us as we are after him. He'd run around the world ten times if he had to, but he'd catch up with the bastards, battle 'em with his bare hands if he had to, and beat 'em. He'd get us back, and all in one piece. We're getting him back the same way, 'we' meaning the three of us. Now, there's a camera fellow's business over there next to the saloon. See the sign? Let's go take your pretty picture.''

The railroad offered the best means of getting from Cheyenne to the Mexican border. Boating the Platte to the Missouri was too roundabout, and the other, more direct rivers and streams were either too shallow in spots or their water disappeared entirely, sinking beneath their sandy beds, flowing underground for some distance and resurfacing as a rivulet or spring. The Rio Grande rose in southern Colorado, entered New Mexico through deep canyons near the center of the northern boundary, and continued flowing southward through the entire territory, but the farther south it wandered the more frequently it dried up. The Pecos, which also flowed southward, wound up in Texas, where it joined the Rio Grande. Unfortunately, it too dried up much to often to be navigable. Traveling from Cheyenne, or even Denver below it, all the way to Mexico on horseback would be much too arduous and time-consuming. Stagecoaches were slow, schedules undependable. The railroad was the only way to go.

On the train eastbound to Cheyenne Doc and Raider decided that spreading Casimir's likeness of the Reverend Strawson about the territories wasn't such a profound idea after all. For one thing, it would bring practically everybody west of the Mississippi into the act. It would immediately alert the agency people as to what had taken place thirteen miles west of Cheyenne and set them into a frenzy of activity that could jeopardize Allan Pinkerton's safety even more than it was jeopardized already. It could also induce his captors to alter his disguise, making distributing the Reverend Strawson's photograph a useless exercise.

One question persistently nagged Doc's allegiance to logic. The people who had abducted the chief, leaving Bolton in his place, had to realize that all he, Doc, and Raider need do would be to hang onto the actor and show him to stationmasters, off-duty conductors, and other train people and ask if they'd seen anyone who resembled him. Reverend Strawson presented a memorable appearance, to say the least: gray hair and beard; clerical collar; and except for his collar, black from hat to boots. It was not your everyday dress in the West. How, then, were Pinkerton's captors escorting him southward? Raider suggested that the chief was sitting between them with a bag over his head. Doc didn't think this funny. Casimir did and laughed and nearly paid dearly for it.

The trio's travel plan was dependent upon the sequence of completed lines that ran southward. A Union Pacific spur covered the 103 miles from Cheyenne to Denver. In Denver they could board the Denver & Rio Grande Western, the "Colorado local," as many of the mine owners and cattle and grain shippers called it. It ran south to Cuchara along the most treacherous and tortuous route east of the Rockies. It required two engines to pull a seven-car string up some of the steepest grades ever railed. It ran along the eastern face on ribbons of steel set more than a foot and a half closer than the standard gauge of four feet, eight and a half inches. The narrow gauge saved time and money when construction called for cutting into solid granite.

Reaching Cuchara, in the southeastern corner of Colorado, the Denver & Rio Grande turned west, slicing through the Culebra Range and dipping down into the narrow San Luis Valley. From there it swung south, twisting its way across the border to Chama.

An off-duty engine wiper, with whom Raider happened to get into conversation while they were waiting for the train to take them down to Denver, suggested that instead of heading west to Chama they could save time by running down to

Trinidad, just below Cuchara, and there change over to the Atchison, Topeka & Santa Fé.

The A.T.&S.F. ran all the way down to El Paso. Opposite El Paso, across the Rio Grande, lay El Paso del Norte, welcome mat to Mexico.

When Raider conveyed this information to Doc as the two Pinkertons and their hostage sat down on board the Cheyenne-Denver train, Raider's expression was as pleased as the Cheshire cat's. Doc darkened it immediately.

"How come you didn't know that in the first place?"

"How come you didn't?"

"You're the one who's supposed to know the territories like the back of your hand, as you keep telling me. Which reminds me. Can't you come up with a different comparison, something not quite as stale?"

"Wiseass. If you must know, I haven't been in this neck o' the woods in two years. Railroads get built fast, you know. New routes spring up up like friggin' toadstools."

"There's no need to make excuses, Rade."

"Who in hell is . . ."

Raider stopped short as two benign-looking nuns slipped by them, heading up the aisle. The whistle blasted, the sound lancing their eardrums; the train jolted, flattening the passengers against the backs of their seats; two pieces of luggage tumbled down from the overhead net racks, and away they went.

"Are you two going snipe at each other all the way to Denver?" asked Bolton, scratching his beard.

"We might if we feel like it, Casimir. What's it to you?" growled Raider.

"Must I sit between you? Is it necessary?"

Doc stared at him. "What do you think?"

"You have my photograph, three of them in fact. Isn't it about time I took off this foolish beard?"

"It wasn't so foolish when they handed you the money to stick it on, was it?" said Raider.

"Take it off," said Doc. "Only hang onto it, and the wig. I'll hold them."

"Thank you." To the astonishment of everyone seated nearby, included the two Sisters of Charity, Bolton began peeling off his beard and rolling off the spirit gum, rubbing his fingers back and forth over his cheeks and chin. He then proceeded to remove his wig, revealing his close-cropped black hair.

"Rade," said Doc, "we've got a small problem."

"Small?"

"I'm not talking about running down to Mexico, I'm talking about money. How much have you got?"

"I don't know, maybe four dollars."

"Great God! All I've got is thirty!"

Raider nudged Bolton with his elbow. "What do you say, Casimir, how's about lending us some?"

"You both saw my wallet. All I have is six or seven dollars."

"I'm not talking about what you're carrying, I mean your bank account."

Bolton blanched. A smile slowly broadened Doc's handsome face, lighting it up like a bull's-eye lantern.

"The man's right, Cas, your blood money's sitting down in Denver in the Miners and Merchants Bank. When we get there, what do you say you walk us over to the bank and make a little withdrawal?"

Raider nodded. "What do you say you close out your account?"

"You two think you're funny, don't you?" responded Bolton. He glowered.

"That's not humor, Casimir," said Doc. "You're an actor—so your notices say, at any rate. Don't you recognize irony when you see it? We need an angel for this little adventure production of ours, and you, mister, are it."

CHAPTER EIGHT

Bolton detested the idea of withdrawing his $2,500 in order to finance the chase. He didn't put it into words, but his expression said all too clearly that he was boiling mad. Now that he'd removed his beard and makeup he looked rather nondescript, apart from his Roman nose, prominent cheekbones, and a cleft in his chin that, fixed on the faces of better-known actors, drove impressionable, stage-struck ladies wild. Along with removing his disguise, he had also changed clothes at the station.

"Smile," advised Raider as the three of them crossed the street and approached the bank. "Be friendly. Look natural. You put it in, you're taking it out. It's that simple."

Doc followed Bolton inside, his arms folded, his right hand gripping his .38 under his jacket.

"May I help you?" inquired the pretty blond cashier, batting her lashes over huge cornflower blue eyes.

Bolton slipped his receipt across the counter. "I'd like to close out my account."

She read the slip, reacting to the size of the amount. "You wish to withdraw the entire amount?"

"Yes."

"But it's only been on deposit six days."

"Miss," he began irritably.

Doc nudged his leg with his knee, persuading him to get a better grip on his self-control.

"I . . . have to leave town unexpectedly. Going back East."

She shoved a slip of paper and a pen toward him. "I'll need your signature."

He sighed "Chad Bolton." She compared the slip with his account application card. The signatures matched to her satisfaction. Standing behind Bolton, Doc got out an Old Virginia cheroot and lit it with a kitchen match. A lady behind him as big as a bale of hay and just as squat looking sniffed and daggered the nape of his neck with her eyes disapprovingly.

"Your address, please?" the cashier asked Bolton.

"Room 2A, Cherokee Hotel."

"Mother's name?"

"Sophia. Father's, Casimir."

Pulling open her cash drawer, she paused. "Any particular denominations?"

Bolton started to turn toward Doc. Again Doc's knee found the back of the actor's leg.

"Twenties and fifties. Maybe a couple tens."

She counted out the money, recounted it, counted it a third time, and pushed the stack toward him.

"Thank you," he said, restoring his fedora to his head and touching the brim. "Good day."

"Good day."

Doc stepped up to the window, doffing his derby. "Afternoon, I'd like to apply for a mortgage loan."

"I'm sorry, sir, the M and M doesn't handle mortages. Try the Colorado National, it's right up the street."

"Thank you, thank you kindly."

Leaving a cloud of smoke to keep the lady behind him company, Doc quick-stepped, catching up with Bolton. Outside the bank Raider approached them.

"How'd it go?" he asked.

Doc smiled. "Silk. Sterling performance, Casimir. You know, you're not a half-bad actor."

Bolton's lip curled as he started to hand him the money. Doc gestured to keep it. "We're not going to be painting the town with it. You be the banker. We'll take it as we need it."

"You're a classic, Weatherbee. Not only do you rob me blind, but you make me hold the money so you can do it gradually, like pulling a sliver out slowly as you can."

"On second thought," said Doc, "better give me fifty for our train fare now."

"I thought Pinkerton operatives rode gratis."

"Some trains, the ones the agency's on retainer with. Not the D.&R.G."

"Speaking of trains, we better shake a leg," said Raider. "We only got about twelve minutes to catch ours. And we should show the picture to the station people before we get on."

"Why bother?" said Doc. "We know they came down this way. We can start showing the picture when we get to Santa Fe."

They crossed the street, dodging traffic, Bolton, as always, walking between them. They rounded a corner into the broad thoroughfare of 16th Street. Denver was growing fast, mushrooming into city size. A gasworks had gone into operation some years earlier, and streetlights stood at every corner. The population had quadrupled in five short years, and everyone seemed to be out today. The sidewalks were mobbed with early-afternoon shoppers. One would have imagined that Christmas was a week away instead of four months.

The three walked on in silence. They turned another corner, coming within sight of the station. Suddenly they heard a high-pitched voice behind them. A boy about ten came running up, his cap awry, his nose runny, his freckled face masked with concern. He tugged at Bolton's sleeve.

"Hey, mister, mister, lookee what you dropped in that trash barrel back there in fronta Dillingbee's!"

He held up the roll of money.

Bolton coughed. "You must be mistak—"

"Give it here," said Raider, snatching it from the boy.

Pedestrians were stopping around them, beginning to hem them in, rubbernecking, murmuring comments.

"Whatcha doin'?" snapped the boy indignantly. "It's this here fella's. He's the one dropped it. I seen him. Reached round behind you and plop into the trash barrel."

Raider handed the money to Bolton, his eyes narrowing menacingly.

"That was careless of you, Cas, old friend," he said.

"Very," added Doc.

Patting the boy on the head, Doc got out a dollar, holding it up with the reverence one might accord Old Glory. Everyone looked on beamed approvingly.

"What's your name, son?"

"Louis."

"Louis, my friends and I thank you. You're an honest citizen. You're going to go far."

Again he patted his head, and handed him the dollar.

"I'd go twice as fur iffin you made it two bucks."

The crowd tittered. A couple of older women made sweet, unsolicited comments. Doc gave Louis a sour look and another dollar. Pushing through the crowd, the three of them continued on toward the station.

"Give me the roll, Casimir," said Doc tightly. "You pull another stunt like that and I promise you it'll cost you a lot more than money."

Bolton sighed and handed Doc the money. "Pity."

Raider threw him an icy glance. "Feeling sorry for yourself again?"

"It's not that. It's the human race. That nosy little ragamuffin. Why can't people mind their own business?"

Raider laughed. Doc laughed. Bolton pouted like a five-year-old and swore softly.

CHAPTER NINE

Bolton's awkward attempt to get rid of the money proved one thing to both Pinkertons: It was an act of desperation. The actor had been insisting all along that they didn't stand a chance of catching up with and rescuing the chief. But now it was clear that Bolton was mortally afraid that they might. And if they did, in the eyes of those who had hired him, he would be guilty of leading Raider and Doc straight to their quarry.

"You know where they're holed up down there," said Raider quietly, following Bolton up the steps and into the car. "You're just worried we'll cash in your chips here and now if you tell us. Right?"

"I haven't the faintest idea where they are. If I've told you once, I've told you twenty times."

What he had told them on the way down from Cheyenne wasn't much help. Four men had been involved in the abduction, including the greasy, potbellied intruder who had "checked out" the berth compartment, opening the barred door to let Bolton in. Where the "doorman" had gotten to in the meantime Bolton had no idea. Like the actor himself, he was only a hired specialist. Bolton did admit knowing about the Clancy brothers and the threatening letters sent to Allan Pinkerton signed Jayhawker Justice. He assured both Pinkertons that the threat would be carried out if the six Clancys went to the gallows. Allan Pinkerton would die.

"You surprise me, Casimir," said Doc as they settled into their seats. "You're still a young man. You're talented, experienced. How could you let yourself get mixed up in this mess?"

"You're holding twenty-four-hundred-and-fifty reasons. Ah me, as Caliban so sagely put it, misery acquaints a man with strange bedfellows."

"I don't think that was Caliban," said Doc. "I think it was Triculo the jester who said it."

"Quite right. Let me ask you a question. You're obviously a man of breeding and education." Bolton paused and eyed Raider, his expression clearly rejecting him from the same classification. Raider returned his look with even deeper disdain. "What in the world are you doing, playing policeman?" continued Bolton to Doc.

"I'm crazy about traveling."

"He's a 'policeman' on account he's damn good at it," said Raider.

Doc smirked. "Thanks, Rade. I never thought I'd hear you—"

"When you're good at something, it stands to reason you stick with it," Raider went on. "Take you, Casimir. If you was really good at stage acting you'd be working steady. The bucks'd be piling in. You wouldn't have to get into crime on the side."

"You don't understand. Treading the boards is an uncertain pursuit. One doesn't become an actor for money, one does it for love of the art, for the music of applause, the plaudits, the immense satisfaction. Ahem, face it: Man does not live by bread alone."

"Cut the horseshit. You'd cut your grandmother's throat for four bucks and you know it!"

"And you, Raider, are contumelious."

Doc chuckled.

Raider's expression in reaction clearly announced that he didn't know the meaning of the word. But criticism is easily recognized by the tone of utterance. His face clouded and he started to respond. A voice interrupted.

"Tickets. Tickets, please."

The conductor looked like a go-back prospector—short, lean, grizzled, with hands as horny and hard-looking as carved rock. He looked ludicrously out of place in his conductor's blues and peaked pillbox cap. He came working his hand punch up the aisle toward them.

"Tickets, tickets . . ."

Doc proffered the fifty-dollar bill. The conductor grunted.

"What the hell you think I am, the Colorado National Bank?"

"It's for the three of us," said Doc.

Again the man grunted. "How far you going?"

"Trinidad."

"The hell you are. Not on this line."

"The man said Trinidad," interposed Raider.

"I heard him, Cowboy Bill. Do you know what train you're on? This here's the D.&R.G. To Castle Rock, Colorado Springs, change for Manitou, to Pueblo, change to Florence and the Canon City–Salida–Leadville spur, Cuchara, spur to La Veta, Russell, Alamosa, Antonito, and Chama. Or straight down from Cuchara to El Moro. No muss, no fuss, no Trinidad, and whoever told you so's a bald-faced liar."

"Our mistake," said Doc. "How close do you run to Trinidad?"

"El Moro, about five miles away. Three big, strapping fellers like you ought to be able to hoof it."

"Give us three to El Moro." Again he held up the fifty-dollar bill.

"Three to El Moro. That'll be fifty-seven bucks."

"Fifty-seven bucks!" exclaimed Raider.

"One-hundred-ninety miles three times. Ten cents a mile. Fifty-seven dollars. This kinda scenery don't come cheap, Cowboy Bill."

"Will you stop calling me—"

Doc laid a hand across Bolton's chest and on Raider's arm. "Rade, please."

The fare was paid, the tickets punched, and the conductor went on his way. Doc got out a folded photograph of Bolton disguised as Reverend Strawson.

"Rade, corner him down in the vestibule and see if he recognizes this."

"I thought you said—"

"I know, but we've got nothing but time from here to El Moro. You might just as well check."

Raider came up behind the conductor, who was standing at the end of the car, thumbing through a handful of greenbacks. He showed him the photograph.

"Ever see this fellow?"

"Sky pilot. Sure."

"When?"

"Couple days back. Let's see." He thought a moment, biting his lip to help bring memory back. "Wednesday. Yup. Today's Friday. It was Wednesday. I had the south run Wednesday, came back yesterday. I remember him. Didn't say nothing to me. Other fellers did all the talking. He just sat staring straight ahead sitting between 'em. Like the fella sitting between you and the fella by the window."

"Did you notice the boys on either side of him?"

"Nope. It was his collar made me look at him. And I recollect the beard."

"What'd the other two look like?"

"Don't remember. You see as many faces as I see, brother, they all blur together, men and women. Like I say, only reason I remember him is the collar. We don't get too many sin busters. They generally stay put wherever they settle down to preaching."

"Do you remember where they were heading?"

"Are you kidding? How the hell would I remember that?"

"Just asking. Thanks."

"Hold on. How come all the questions? Who is this fella?"

"Reverend Weatherbee."

"How come you're asking after him? Carrying round his picture?"

"Well, it's kinda' embarrassin'. Us three go to his church, and a pile o' church funds are missing, and he lit out."

"Oh boy, ain't that something! If you can't trust a sky pilot, who in hell can you? Course, they're only human. Hope you catch up with him."

"So do we. So does the Men's Club and the Ladies' Aid Society. Thanks."

•   •   •

The D.&R.G. was known as the Baby Road, its trains riding on skinnier than standard rails, weighing only thirty pounds a yard and set only three feet apart. The little engines, weighing only twelve and a half tons, burned inferior but expensive coal extracted from the fields of northern Colorado—one of the reasons why the Baby Road charged an exorbitant ten cents a mile. Knowledgeable railroad people claimed that freight could be transported more cheaply from New York to Denver than from Denver to Pueblo on the D.&R.G., a distance of only 118 miles.

The conductor's comment on the scenery was not without truth. It was magnificent; it was also frightening, particularly to Doc, who was seated by the window and able to look straight down into granite gorges a thousand feet deep. Rumor had it that the D.&R.G.'s cars were only permitted one coat of paint; two coats, and the top one would be scraped off by the wall of rock along which the twin-engined trains crawled. The heights were awesome; the closeness of the facing of the Rampart Range rock opposite scary; the roadbed spongy, the train at times jolting and shaking so, everyone on board, including the conductor, had to grab whatever was close and solidly anchored and hang on white-knuckled and ashen-cheeked.

Mountain railroading, it was claimed, was the effort, the obsession of madmen. And surely the maddest, at least the most daring, had to be General William Jackson Palmer, father of the D.&R.G. Building through the ranges was murderously difficult, slow, and costly; riding the lines constructed was classifiable in the opinions of some as group death wishing. In winter the little Rio Grande trains were often buried to above the windows by snows mantling the higher passes. Rounding treacherous curves in the best weather, engineers often came upon twenty-ton boulders that had plunged down canyon walls. During the spring floods, washouts thundered down chasms and ravines, leaving the twisted wreckage of miles of track and cross ties strung in midair. With the curves tight and blind, the grades steep and frequently insurmountable in wet weather, the descents unbrakeable, firing the flanges to white-hot intensity in a sometimes vain effort to hold heavily loaded cars on the rails, life on the Baby Road was nothing if not exciting. Life insurance for his train crews cost Palmer a fortune, one more reason why his freight and passenger rates were so high.

By the time they had reached Pueblo, temporarily abandoning the heights and descending to the plain, night had come to Colorado. Further conversation with the conductor elicited the reason why the D.&R.G. had not laid rails into Trinidad. The residents had expected it to; coal fields lay beneath the town, promising fuel both cheaper and more readily available for the line's locomotives' insatiable fireboxes. But upon departing Cuchara, instead of moving on to Trinidad, the D.&R.G. set up a new town on a large tract of company-owned land five miles northeast of Trinidad.

Trinidadians were enraged, but there was nothing they could do about it beyond writing letters of protest to the governor and occasionally sabotaging the Rio Grande's rails leading into El Moro. Eventually their problem was solved when the Atchison, Topeka & Santa Fe, known locally as the latter only, came into Trinidad.

Arriving in El Moro at close to two o'clock in the morning, Raider and Doc found the local livery stable. As expected, it was in darkness. Raider began knocking, then banging loudly on the door of the house beside it. The disturbance set the stallions inside the stable whinnying protest. Raider continued pounding.

"Hey in there!"

An upstairs window flew open; the barrel of a shotgun emerged. The barrel angled downward. A single blast kicked gravel up three inches from Raider's left boot. A voice bellowed out of the darkness.

"Now ged der hell oud uff here und led a man ged zum schleep!"

Down came the window.

"Nice try, Rade," said Doc.

"Let's walk it," said Raider calmly, stifling a cavernous

yawn with his forearm. "Conductor said its southwest o' here. Let's find the road."

Bolton dipped his knees to pick up his bags, then paused, straightening.

"Aren't we overlooking something?" he asked, looking from one to the other. "That chap upstairs has a point. Isn't it time we ourselves knit up the raveled sleeve of care?"

Raider eyed Doc questioningly.

"Hamlet wants to catch a little shut-eye, Rade."

"You can sleep while you're walking, Casimir. It's only five miles. You ought to be able to do that bowing and applauding yourself all the way."

El Moro continued as black as the inside of a hat in use, in spite of the shotgun blast and the stridently delivered advice that had followed it. In the heavens the North Star hung in place roughly halfway between the Big Dipper and Cassiopeia's Chair. Putting the North Star behind their right shoulders, they started down the slender road toward Trinidad to the southwest. Directly ahead, Purgatory River snaked between the two towns, descending from its source near Trinchera Peak. Reaching the river and finding the bridge collapsed in the middle of it, they waded across.

They walked on in silence, putting the dark outline of El Moro farther and farther behind. They had covered more than half the distance when specks of light began showing on a hilly site ahead. Trinidad, much larger than El Moro, was laid out on both sides of the river near a canyon at the base of a crowd of mountains surrounding Stonewall Valley.

"They look to be still up and drinking in Trinidad," commented Raider. He glanced over his left shoulder at Bolton who was three steps behind, carrying his carpetbag and a large suitcase as if each of them were packed with bricks, with one more added at every step. "How you doing, Cas?"

"Can we stop and rest a few minutes?"

"We're only halfway. Not even three miles."

"Let him rest," said Doc. "We need him in decent shape."

Bolton sniffed. "I'm going to catch my death of never-get-over from wading across that filthy river. I'm still soaking."

"Out here men wear boots, even peewees like Mr. Weatherbee's," said Raider, "not ballroom-dancing shoes like them you got on."

Bolton had sat down by the side of the road near a sprawling clump of scruffy shad scale which appeared to flourish in the sandy soil of the area. He had taken off his shoes and socks and was wringing the water out of one trouser leg, which he had pulled up to his knee. Suddenly the bush to his right shifted. Raider noticed it move.

"Hey, watch it!"

Bolton looked up with a puzzled expression. Out of the bush came a soft, thrashing sound.

"My God!"

A sidewinder a yard long came sidling out, moving swiftly, blundering against Bolton's outstretched bare right leg. He screamed at the contact, kicking, jerking about violently. The snake, aroused, struck, sinking its fangs into the front of Bolton's exposed leg just under the knee.

He screamed and screamed, kicking and pulling himself backwards. Raider drew and fired in one motion, the slug finding sand close to the writhing snake. It released its grip, raising its head, the horns above its jet black eyes erect. Raider's second shot smashed against its head, all but slicing it completely from the body. The fangs dripping venom, the head hung by a flap of skin. Bolton scrambled clear, continuing to scream. The snake dropped, its pink body writhing, flipping over, the flap joining its severed head tearing loose. The body continued twisting, contorting. Raider ran to it, cursing, kicking it into the bush from which it had emerged. Doc knelt beside Bolton, examining the bite by the faint light of the quarter moon. The stricken man had stopped screaming and was moaning and gasping, as if trying to catch his breath.

"How bad?" Raider asked.

Doc frowned. "It's hard to tell."

"Lemme see." Raider got down on his knees, squinted at the twin punctures, and gently pinched the flesh. Twin freshets of blood gushed upward, drenching his hand.

"It's into the goddamn artery!"

Doc had his handkerchief out, winding it hurriedly and casting about, looking for a stick. There was none in sight.

"Pull off part of the bush. I need a stick."

"What the hell for? What the hell good is a tourniquet going to do?" Raider was suddenly enraged. "I tell you it's the artery. Look at the blood. *Look!*"

Doc pulled loose a branch and applied the tourniquet, tightening it, holding it tight, then slowly releasing it.

"Let it bleed! Let it bleed!" snapped Raider.

"He'll bleed to death."

"He won't. Chrissake, do like I tell you."

Shouldering Doc to one side bodily, he pulled off the tourniquet and squeezed the wound, crimsoning his hands. Bolton roared in pain.

"Good Lord, look." Supporting himself with one arm after being pushed over, Doc pointed with his free hand. Other sidewinders, heads raised, were poised looking at them from just behind the bush, less than fifteen feet away. Two came sidling swiftly toward them.

Raider cursed. Picking up Bolton, he whirled on Doc. "Grab the stuff!"

"What about his shoes and—"

"Fuck 'em! Chrissakes *move!*"

"He's lost a lot of blood and a lot of venom with it. All of it, I imagine," said the doctor.

He was young, gangling, with huge hands, and feet that looked to Raider like size sixteens. He was bald and also bleary-eyed, but remarkably good-natured for one who had been awakened two hours before dawn by two strangers, one carrying a barefoot man as white as chalk, a tourniquet wrapped just under his knee, twisted and held in place by a belt.

Raider sat in a chair against the wall looking on. Doc stood beside the doctor. Bolton lay on the examining table in the center of the small room. The office was located over a saloon. Below them the muffled sounds of laughter and a piano being cruelly abused could be heard. Welcome to

Trinidad, open all night, mused Raider grimly. His arms felt as if they'd been pulled a full two inches out of their sockets; his shoulders felt fractured. He had carried Bolton two and a half miles, holding him like a child, draping him over one shoulder, then the other, piggybacking him. He felt compassion for the man, something he would never have thought possible. Their bodies touching as he carried him, he had imagined he could actually feel the life draining out of the man.

He himself could not recall ever feeling so exhausted; he was totally drained. Had he been required to carry Bolton up two more stairs, his knees would most certainly have buckled. Doc, struggling along, carrying Bolton's bags and their own things, had repeatedly offered to swap burdens. Raider had refused to. What, after all, was the point in exchanging a hundred-pound rock for a hundred-pound anvil?

"Will he live?" asked Doc.

The doctor smiled grimly. "He might fool us and do just that." He was trying to relieve the tension, push back the unseen phantom hovering over the table. Bolton looked dead. He did not, could not move, reflected Raider, eyeing him. He himself could scarcely move. If only he could cast off his shoulders, arms and all, and grow new ones instantly. Every part from his fingers up, over to and including his neck, felt broken.

"I don't mean to be facetious," said the doctor. "It has been a long time, dangerously long. If I could have gotten him—"

"He's gonna kick," said Raider mechanically.

"I didn't say that. With snakebite, even without treatment, mortality only runs ten to fifteen percent. Unfortunately, entry *was* directly into the peroneal artery. Extremely heavy loss of blood, although the tourniquet helped. Saved his life, up to now."

"What woulda happened if we kept it on tight? I mean on accounta so much blood, never loosened it."

"At the very least I'd had to have taken his leg off. Look,

there's no sense either of you wasting worrying time looking for alternatives.''

"We coulda seared it," offered Raider.

"You could have washed it with tobacco juice, whiskey, kerosene. If you'd happened to be packing potassium permanganate, you could have used that." He shook his head. "None of them do the slightest good. Because the mortality rate's so low, all such treatments get credit they don't deserve. Not by a damn shot."

Bolton groaned.

"Easy, friend," said the doctor. "He needs blood. Right away."

"How about a transfusion?" asked Doc.

The doctor reacted in mild surprise. "You know about blood transfusion?"

"I know it's the latest thing."

"And it works. They're using it in the hospitals back East. Unfortunately, I don't have the equipment, the necessary pump assembly with the suction cup for the donor." He was talking to the wall, his voice suddenly wistful, his expression helpless. He looked down at Bolton. "We'll get some beef broth into him. One of you go downstairs and get Sheehy to cook some up. He's probably drunk as a lord by now, but if he's not out cold he'll do it."

"If he's out cold, I'll wake him," said Raider, rising wearily.

"I'll go Rade."

"You'd better prepare it," said the doctor. "The bartender'll give you the beef."

Luck was with all three. Bolton recovered, but it was two full days before he showed signs of regaining his strength. His color gradually came back. It was six days before he was able to resume traveling.

They boarded the A.T.&S.F. to Santa Fe, 183 miles distant. The loss in time was more than unfortunate. Much more. It threatened to be disastrous.

CHAPTER TEN

WHERE IS ALLAN PINKERTON?

*Allan Pinkerton, founder and chief of the famed Pin-
kerton National Detective Agency, is missing. Chief Pinkerton left Chicago, Illinois, headquarters of the agency,
en route to San Francisco, where the Pinkertons are
opening a new branch office. The chief planned to officiate at the ceremonies and had also scheduled a side trip
to nearby Oakland, where he was to address a conven-
tion of California law officers.*

*Chief Pinkerton was last seen in the company of two of
his men, Operatives Weatherbury and Raynor, on the
U.P. Transcontinental Train approximately 13 miles west
of Cheyenne, Wyoming. The train had derailed at that
point; according to witnesses at the scene, a tree struck
by lightning had fallen across the tracks. Fortunately,
none of the passengers nor any of the crew suffered
serious injury in the accident. Engineer Buford Cum-
mings saw the tree, but was unable to stop the train in
time. Help was summoned from Cheyenne and arrived
shortly. The train was restored to the tracks and later
continued on its way to Ogden, Utah.*

*Letters threatening Chief Pinkerton with death had been
received at the agency's main offices at 191–193 Fifth
Avenue in Chicago prior to Pinkerton's departure. As a
consequence, he was traveling to San Francisco in disguise.
Reporters requesting details from Mr. William Wagner,
superintendent of the Chicago office, were repeatedly*

told "no comment," but passengers traveling on the same train obliged the press with some information. A Mr. Amos Hunterford of Omaha, Nebraska, recounted a conversation he had had with a fellow passenger shortly before the train passed through Cheyenne. According to Mr. Hunterford, senior partner in the law firm of Hunterford, Hunterford, Hunterford and Drescher in Omaha, the passenger informed him that Chief Pinkerton was traveling disguised as a clergyman. Mr. Hunterford was not certain as to the specific faith, but "had an idea it was Roman Catholic." He himself did not see Chief Pinkerton in disguise, but his informant claimed that earlier in the trip he had shared the chief's sleeping compartment and that he had recognized Pinkerton from his photograph in the Omaha World-Tribune.

Neither Conductor Andrew Murphy or Trainman Clyde Van Husen were aware that Pinkerton and his men were among their passengers. Both employees did however acknowledge that all three occupants of the parlor car coupled to the tender were no longer on board when the train reached Ogden. They further informed reporters that there was no evidence of foul play in the car occupied by Weatherbury, Raynor, and their chief.

Although representatives of the Detective Agency persist in refusing to answer questions, other law enforcement officers have offered explanations regarding the apparent abduction. It is believed that friends of the notorious Clancy brothers gang, all six of whom have been indicted for murder and are presently incarcerated in the State Penitentiary at Lincoln, Nebraska, kidnapped Chief Pinkerton and his bodyguards. It has also been suggested that Weatherbury and Raynor were in on the kidnapping and assisted in its apparently successful execution.

"I'll be a son of a bitch!" snarled Raider.

"Sssh," said Doc. "There's more." He turned to page four of the Santa Fe *New Mexican*.

All six Clancy brothers questioned at the penitentiary deny any knowledge of the situation. However, it is known that their father, Will Francis Clancy, is still at large and is believed responsible for the threatening letters sent to Chief Pinkerton and signed Jayhawker Justice.

Clancy Senior is originally from Cawker City, Kansas, where the family lived for many years. The letters threatening Chief Pinkerton demanded that Governor Garber of Nebraska free all six Clancy brothers or "Allan Pinkerton will be kilt (sic)." The governor's response to the threat has been widely publicized. Said he, "I refuse to knuckle under to threats of any kind from any quarter."

The question in law enforcement circles seems to be why has "Jayhawker Justice" selected Pinkerton as its victim in trying to pressure Governor Garber into releasing the Clancys. Pinkerton's career as a crime fighter has been long and colorful, and it has been suggested that at some time in the distant past he personally or one of his sons had locked horns with the Clancys. However, agency personnel in Chicago and elsewhere have refused to confirm or deny this possibility. At this writing no record has been found of any tie-up between the Pinkertons and the Clancys.

But where is Allan Pinkerton? The train he was on arrived in Oakland on schedule and the passengers moved on to San Francisco by ferry.

Superintendent Wagner has announced that the agency is offering a reward of $25,000 for information leading to the arrest and conviction of Pinkerton's kidnappers.

Outside the hotel room windows the late afternoon shower appeared to be letting up. Beyond a cluster of squat little adobe buildings they could see the plaza surrounded by a platoon of newly installed standards crowned with four-sided, glass-enclosed gas lanterns. No one was about; the usual loiterers and shoppers had taken refuge from the downpour. Rain fell late practically every September afternoon in and around Santa Fe, thunder detonating and occasional lightning flashes ripping the flock of slate gray sheep clouds assembled overhead.

On the narrow bed Bolton slept soundly, his face white with the weakness that still lingered. The train ride out of Trinidad over the 7,800-foot saddle of Raton Pass, across the border, and down to Santa Fe had been tiring for all three; for Bolton it had been exhausting beyond description.

Raider was furious.

"Those bastards! Imagine, accusing us o' snatching him!"

"And misspelling our names to boot."

"You're funny as hell."

"Rade, we've got to do something we've been holding off on." Doc's voice trailed off. He shook his head.

"Yeah? Yeah?"

"We've got to send a telegram to Chicago."

"Are you nuts?"

"Ssssh! Keep your voice down. You'll wake Bolton."

"Fuck him! He's the one got us into this thing."

"And will get us out if we treat him properly, keep him alive and reasonably fit."

Raindrops raced one another down the windowpane to the sill, leaving perpendicular tracks that to Doc in his present mood resembled bars in a cell window.

"He's our only hope. If by some miracle we do catch up with them, we might be able to switch him for the chief. All he'd have to do is put his disguise back on. Then we knock him cold. Make it look like he's sleeping. Give us time to get out, get clear."

"Are you listening to what you're saying? You're talking like an idiot!"

"They did it to us. It's possible we could pull the same thing on them."

"That'd be two miracles: finding him, and getting him out without a scratch. I don't believe in miracles. Not in bunches, not one at a time, no way. We're already six days behind the bastards. I told you in Trinidad, what we shoulda done was you stay there and keep an eye on him and I keep going."

"Isn't this thing complicated enough without making it worse? That's all our splitting up would have done."

"All I know is we're behind by six fuckin' days. Sometimes I think he let that snake bite him on purpose. Hell, they could be clear down to Guatemala by now!"

"Make that seven days. We should stay over here at least a day. Look at him. He's not fit to travel. Not all the way to El Paso. How far is it?"

Raider sighed defeatedly. "Better than three hundred, a lot better. Closer to three fifty. Thirteen, fourteen hours, maybe more. We could run into another tree across the tracks, get stopped by Apaches, held up by renegades . . ."

"My, but we're in a pleasant mood today, aren't we?"

"What in hell have any of us got to be pleasant about? Besides, it's goddamn raining. Rain always gets me down. And my back hurts from sitting in that damn train, and I'm hungry and tired."

"The rain's stopping. The sun's coming out. About the telegram . . ."

"Doc, why? You spill the beans to big-mouth Wagner and every Pink within a thousand miles'll be hightailing it down to El Paso. They'll swarm into Mexico like buffalo gnats. Word'll get back to old man Clancy or whoever's holding the chief, and from then on it'll be hell with the hide off."

"Will you let me speak? I just want Chicago to know we're hot on the trail."

"Shit!"

Bolton stirred.

"Keep it down," muttered Doc, annoyed.

"Hot on the trail, that's a laugh."

"We can be, with a little luck, a break or two. Properly worded, Wagner won't alert anybody. He won't be able to. He won't know where to send them. Rade, Mrs. Pinkerton is sitting back there worrying herself sick, imagining he's already dead."

"He most likely is."

Doc folded the newspaper and tossed it into a corner.

"You know better than that. As long as the Clancy boys are alive, this Jawhawker scum will keep *him* alive."

"I got a feeling from that newspaper that the Clancys aren't going to be round much longer. That governor up in Nebraska is already winding the noose. He as good as says in that paper he doesn't care whether A.P. lives or dies."

"What the paper says he says and what he actually thinks could be two different things. It won't hurt him in the slightest to hold off their execution. Trust me, I promise I'll work out the wording very, very carefully. All I'll say is that we're hot on the trail, we have inside information as to where they're holding the chief, and we'll be in touch as soon as we have more to report. I'll tell him things look good."

"Things look great."

"It's hogwash, I admit, but it'll ease the poor woman's mind. It'll also tell Wagner that the two of us are above suspicion. You know what it says in the paper."

"Screw the paper. Wagner no more thinks we're in on kidnapping him than the man in the moon. We maybe messed things up, but we didn't help engineer the thing. Oh hell, if you want to send a telegram, go ahead, but if we get to El Paso and walk smack into a crowd o' Pinks and Billy Pinkerton all set to hand us our heads, don't go saying I didn't warn you." He stretched out on his bed. "You do like you please. Me, I'm getting some shut-eye."

Doc stood up, glanced at the sleeping Bolton, and lowered his voice. "When I leave, make sure you lock the door and hide the key under your pillow or wherever. The last thing we need is for him to wake up, spot you asleep, and sneak out of here. He wouldn't hesitate to try it."

"Yeah, yeah."

Doc left. Raider locked the door behind him, tested it, then kicked off his boots, lay down, and slipped the key under his pillow. Looking over at Bolton in the corner bed, he reassured himself that the actor was still fast asleep and closed his eyes.

The rain had stopped, but it still fell from the edge of the roof, splashing softly on the outside sill. He fell asleep and began dreaming of the Birdcage Theatre in Tombstone. What a flashy place, great waterhole, exciting, all kinds of action going on round the clock. He could hear the clicking of the roulette ball through the babble and laughter and the piano.

She was standing at the top of the stairs to the left, all satin and sequins and ruffles, black on pink, and with a pretty feather in her chestnut hair. Under the feather she wore a sort of net wrapped around like a headband with sparkly things on it. She was tall and pretty with a beautiful mouth, high cheekbones, and dark skin, like she had Mexican or Indian blood.

She saw him and smiled and started down, the sequins in her black stockings glittering as they caught the glow of the overhead lamps. Buy me a drink, she was going to say when she came up to him, and she did. He did. Whiskey. She bolted it down like it was lemon squash. They talked. The sounds surrounding them, the jangly piano, muffled their conversation. The air was thick with tobacco smoke and smelled foul. It was close and uncomfortably warm. Tiny beads of sweat glistened at the tops of her breasts. She caught him looking and smiled. She had such a great smile, so friendly and inviting, and she liked him. He could always tell, mostly by how easy it was to talk right off the bat, the way they prattled on like they were old friends meeting.

There were no tables free, and the bar was crowded four deep. They went outside for air, still jabbering away. She walked him around the back of the building and up the stairs. The door at the top was locked, but she had a key on a silver chain around her neck. She held his hand, leading him down a narrow hallway through the darkness. They could hear the carrying-on downstairs, but it sounded strange, like it was miles beneath their feet instead of right under them.

They were in bed naked as jays fresh out of their shells, lying in darkness, wrapped in some flowery scent, lilac or lavender, violet, tuberose, he couldn't tell what, never had been able to, didn't much care. They knotted together, pressing close, hard, her nipples hard as quarters riveted against his chest. He ran his free hand down the arch of her back to the cleavage of her buttocks. Her skin was soft as rose petals, starting tiny fires in the tips of his fingers. She began fumbling, finding his cock, her hand sliding down it to his balls, caressing them gently, tenderly.

Erection came in seconds.

"Rade! *Rade!*"

It was a knife coming down from above, ripping the scene in half like it was a painted backdrop on a stage, slicing it so that the two halves fell away, crumpling, leaving a thick gray cloud.

"Rade!"

He woke, his mouth tasting foul, his tongue thickened with it, like it was wrapped with wool. He licked his lips. He glanced up hazy-eyed, expecting Doc to be standing over him.

He wasn't. The fog in his mind cleared, the dream came back. Lying with her in her room up over the Birdcage, Doc had interrupted them, come bursting in, calling his name, shouting. Something had happened down the street.

He touched his temples, scowling, trying to recall. He couldn't.

His eyes drifted to the door. It stood ajar. He threw a glance at Bolton, sleeping in the corner. The bed was empty, the thin blanket and sheet beneath it messed. Both his bags were gone. Raider cursed, shoving his hand under his pillow. The key was gone.

He jumped up, toeing his feet into his boots, rushing to the window. A few people were in the plaza. The sun had gone back in, restoring the gloominess that had prevailed during the downpour. Under the thick boughs of the cottonwood trees surrounded by a white picket fence in the center of the plaza dark shadows draped the empty bandstand.

He spotted Bolton emerging from between two buildings, entering the plaza, walking fast, a bag in each hand, doing splendidly for a sick man.

"Bastard!"

Snatching up his gunbelt, he ran out, down four flights to the narrow street. He ran between identical sun-baked brick houses with identical narrow inset doorways topped by six-inch-wide lintels. He met no one, saw no one until he came into the plaza. Directly ahead stood the palace, its long portals supported by evenly spaced square pillars painted a brilliant white. A low white balustrade of wooden pegs with, over them, white wooden urns aligned with the pillars below, belted the facade like icing on a cake. The other three sides of the plaza were lined with covered walks. Streets led away from them.

Bolton had disappeared down one. Which? he wondered, seething, furious with himself for his carelessness.

Toward the railroad station. He would catch the first train out, riding it until the conductor came along and asked for his ticket. He wouldn't have one, wouldn't have the money to buy one. They'd put him off the train. First stop, Lamy. At Lamy the main line picked up. He could board another train, this time heading north, pull the same stunt. . . .

There probably wouldn't be a train for at least an hour, maybe longer. He'd realize that and hide out someplace near the station. If he was smart, nowhere near it, better far over the other side of town. But he was anxious, desperate to get away from them, to get free of the trap his greed for the $2,500 had sprung on him. He'd hide out near the station.

Raider ran down the walkway, gaining the street heading in the direction of the station. The street ran straight as wire. Eighty to a hundred yards ahead he spotted Bolton, slowed considerably by his condition and the weight of his bags. Bolton stopped and set them down; flexed his fingers; drew a deep breath.

Raider ran swiftly, closing the distance that separated them. He came up to within fifty yards of him, his hand going to his .45. He was about to call out, order him to stop, when two men came out of a side street, positioning themselves almost exactly midway between Raider and the actor. Raider ducked into a doorway as both turned to look back. Then they looked at the actor. One was a head taller than the other, bigger through the body, fat. In his left hand was a gun.

Raider pulled his .45. Too late. The man fired. The sound

was like dynamite going off. Bolton's arms flew outward at right angles to his body. His death yell started, was cut short. He fell to his knees and forward onto his face hard.

Raider fired, dropping the killer. The man with him swung about. Anxious faces, huge eyes, gaping mouths appeared in windows and doorways—women, children, an old man . . .

"Stop right there or you're dead!" called Raider.

The man ducked and threw himself to one side, vanishing between the buildings the same way he had come out. Raider fired twice and missed. He ran to the corner and swung around it. The man was up on his horse, spurring it cruelly, digging his rowels deep. The horse whinnied in pain, tensed, and flung itself down the street.

Raider ran up to the hitch rack. Flipped around it were the reins of the other man's horse. Raider loosened them, mounted, and thundered off in pursuit.

The street widened gradually, the buildings slipping behind them; they were out of town, heading west. Raider got off a third shot, but the horse ahead did not slow. Three shots left. He dug his spurless heels into his horse, lowering in the saddle; the horse flew forward with renewed energy, a good horse, he thought, big brush-tailed bay, strong, power to burn, a love-to-run horse, pulling forward faster, closing the gap.

Curly mesquite and yucca and cactus sprang up on both sides of the muddy road. The land swelled away toward the dove gray sky, the varying shades of plant green darkened by the cloud cover hiding the sun.

Raider soon closed to within clear, easy shooting distance. He let one go. The horse ahead tried to brake too suddenly. It stumbled and almost fell. The rider reined up. Raider came coasting up alongside. The man raised his hands. He wasn't wearing a gun.

"I got no gun."

"I can see, you bastard."

He was bleeding from the shoulder. One of Raider's two street shots had found its mark.

"I'm hurtin' real bad. I think my shoulder's busted." His hand went to it, and he grimaced in pain.

He was ugly, mused Raider, his nose fist-flattened against his face. His face looked as if it had been slapped too hastily against his head, twisted slightly to one side; the left side of his mouth hung down, aggravating the impression. His skin was so dark under the brim of his Stetson it looked black. But he was no Negro, and not Mexican or Indian.

He had a whiny voice, an annoying singsong tone—natural or for effect, for sympathy. Whatever the cause, the sound of it soured Raider.

"You killed Jephtha," he said, his face dropping as if he were about to start crying.

"I'll kill you, you bastard."

"I didn't do nothin'. I couldn't. You can see, I ain't got no gun, no knife, nothing. You wouldn't kill a unarmed man."

"I'll kill you in two winks if you don't shut up. Turn your horse around, we're going back."

"Man, we can't. That'd be loco!"

"Do it, goddamn it!"

He did so. Raider followed him back to town at a lope, keeping three lengths behind, his gun restored to its holster. About a quarter of a mile from the spot where the fleeing man had stopped, he again reined up.

"What's the matter now?" Raider asked.

His ire had come to a rolling boil. Bolton. The bastard must have swiped the key out from under his pillow like a magician pulling a rabbit out of a hat, easy as breathing, slick as a waxed bar. Doc would be furious, and had every right to be. He should have stuck the goddamn key in his crotch under his nuts. Let Casimir try to swipe it then.

Now the stupid son of a bitch was dead, their last hope with a slug in his pump, his lungs full of blood. Dead as the snake that bit him. And for what? Twenty-five hundred stinking dollars.

"Goddamn son of a bitch! What do you want, you bastard!"

The man paled, then back came the pleading look that matched his voice so well.

"It's my shoulder, it's bad busted."

"It is like hell. The hit's not high enough up. It's a good two inches from the bone."

"Can't you do something to help stanch the bleedin'?"

"It's just a trickle. It's cleaning it for you."

"We got to get the slug out else I'll get the mortification for sure. I could easy lose my arm." He pulled his shirt up from the wound, freeing it from the clotting. He winced with pain, stuck his finger in the hole in the material, ripped it. "Be Christian, man. At least look at it, see how bad it is. It's terrible bad, I can feel it."

"I can't feel nothing. You can tell better'n me. You'd love me to lean close so you could haul me down and maybe bust my neck hitting the ground. You'd be down on me like a shot, shoulder or no."

"You got me wrong, mister. I know when I'm beat."

"Get down off your horse."

"What you gonna do? I thought you said . . ."

"Down."

They both dismounted. Raider drew his gun. "Empty your pockets."

"I can't got nothin', honest. A few bucks, some pesos . . ."

"Empty 'em."

He complied. He had no wallet. He had eight dollars and change and about thirty dollars worth of paper pesos.

"That it?"

"Every cent I got, honest. It's all yours."

"I'm not robbing you, you asshole. All I want is for the law to string you up."

He gasped. "What for? I ain't done nothin'. You saw . . ."

"You call accomplice to murder nothing? Oh man, you're gonna swing all right. Turn out your shirt pocket."

"Why? There's nothin' . . ."

"Turn it out!"

Pay dirt. A newspaper picture of Bolton, wearing a wig and a ruff around his neck, his eyes darkened by heavy makeup, but there was no mistaking that face.

"Good boy."

"My shoulder!"

"One more goddamn word about your shoulder and I swear I'll shoot it off and make you chew on it!" Raider's eyes flicked back and forth between the picture and his captive. "It's just like I figured, and this proves it. You two come up to get him, and you got him. Simple as that, right?"

Like the headlight of an oncoming locomotive, a thought flashed through his mind. "Up? Or down? You two been on our tails, right?"

"No, sir."

Raider lifted the muzzle of his gun slowly, aiming at the other's face. The man swallowed, paling visibly. He looked as if he was suddenly sick to his stomach.

"Tell me about it."

"Jep and me come up from El Paso."

"Jep and who?"

"Me."

"Don't you have a name?"

"Artis. Artis Thatcher. Artis Henry Thatcher, after my daddy."

"Okay, Artis Henry Thatcher, after your daddy, you came up from Mexico. Where, exactly? Let's have it straight, I'm asking one time only. Where'bouts your pals got the old man?"

"Chihuahua."

"Where in Chihuahua."

"Near to Rosales. It's just a place, it ain't got a name."

"Good boy, now we're gettin' somewheres. Old man Clancy's holding him, right?" Thatcher hesitated, then nodded. "Hostage. To keep the governor of Nebraska from hanging the family."

Again Thatcher nodded, then bit his lower lip and threw back his head as if he'd caught a lance squarely in the spine. His shoulder again, thought Raider. He was wrong.

"God Almighty, Almighty, Almighty. I'm gonna' get myself kilt for what I'm tellin' you."

"You can get that just for riding with killers, in this case gutless bastards who specialize in shooting people in the back. One more question. For now. What's Clancy's beef against Allan Pinkerton?''

"I don't know.''

"The hell you don't. You got ears.''

"I swear I don't! All I know's what one o' the boys said he *thought*. Just thought, mind you. But then he's one mighty smart thinker.''

"Get on with it.''

"Dabs Cruikshank. He says Will Francis picked on Pinkerton 'cause he's Mr. Big Badge, you know, the big lawdog, the biggest. He's like a . . . what do you call it?''

"Symbol. He symbolizes the law.''

"That's the word, I think.''

"Okay. Now, instead o' me turning' you in so they can string you up, I'm gonna be big hearted. You've earned yourself a temporary reprieve. You got yourself a job. You're gonna escort me and my partner on down there.''

"Oh, God Almighty, Almighty, don't make me do that. Clancy'd cut me in half with his shotgun.''

"Talk to him nice, act friendly, maybe he'll go easy on you.'' Raider paused, fish-eyeing him. "You're a Jayhawker.''

"Yes, sir.''

"Cawker City.''

"Nope. Near to Glen Elder, just up the tracks.''

"You and the Clancys kin?''

"Way back.''

"Okay, like I say, you're takin' us back with you. You, me, and my partner'll take the train down to El Paso, cross over, head through the mountains, down across the Rio Conchos. How far from there?''

"A long ways.''

Raider snickered. "Two jumps and a half, I bet.''

"I'll never make it, not with this shoulder.''

"You'll make it. By the time we get there you'll be back doin' cartwheels. My partner's a doctor. He'll dig a little hole in you, I'll hold you upside down by the ankles, and that slug'll drop out slick as you please.''

"You wouldn't hurt me, God Almighty . . ." He gaped. Raider held every muscle in his face steady, hard-eyeing him. "You are plumb heartless. Ain't you got no human feelings?"

"You bet. For human beings. Mount up."

CHAPTER ELEVEN

Doc was more than furious; when Raider tried to explain what had happened in his partner's absence, Doc reacted as if he'd suddenly gone insane. For a few frightening seconds Raider thought he'd rip every hair out of his head, or attack him. First one, then the other. Artis Thatcher sat on Bolton's bed, staring at Doc's performance in patent disbelief, his free hand holding a wet towel against his wound.

"What I don't understand is how Casimir knew where to look for the key."

Doc stopped pacing and glared at him fiercely. "He heard every word we said, that's how!"

"How could he, he was asleep."

"He was pretending. The man was an actor. He heard, he saw everything."

"Well, you're the one said I should stick the key under my pillow. It wasn't my idea."

"You're the loudmouth who woke him up. I kept telling you and telling you to keep it down."

"You said—"

"Kindly shut up, will you. I'm trying to think."

Thatcher's subdued voice came from the corner. "You two on the same side?" he asked.

"You shut up," snapped Raider.

"I'm sorry," He moaned. "I'm hurtin' real bad, fellas. I'm sufferin'."

Doc calmed down. "He needs a doctor."

"He told me you was a doctor, you could take out this

80

slug. I'm getting the mortification. I am for sure. It's settin' in, I can feel it.''

"Just calm down," said Doc. "We'll get you taken care of." He turned back to Raider, his face masked with disgust. "I don't believe this. I leave you alone for half an hour, less, and the whole circus blows up. Bolton's killed, you gun down somebody with half of Sant Fe looking on, and then bring this one back all shot to pieces. I don't suppose it occurred to you to sneak him up the back way, keep clear of the lobby.''

"Weatherbee, you think you're so smart, you got all the answers. There ain't no goddamn back way! There's back ways to firehouses, whorehouses, every house but a doghouse, but not hotels on account if there was, people would sneak out without paying. Don't you know that? Don't you know any damn thing?''

"All right, all right. Only bringing him through a lobby full of people . . .''

"There weren't more than two, sittin' with their noses in their newspapers, and the old lady behind the desk. She didn't see beans. She sure didn't see he was hurtin'.''

"How do you know she didn't?''

"She didn't say nothin'. She woulda at least made a face and gaped or something. Besides, what else could I do but bring him up here? You rather I run him over to the station to wait for the train? How would I let you know? What was I supposed to do, tie him to one o' the platform stanchions and run and get you? I had to bring him up!''

Doc was looking at his watch. "I checked on the way back from Western Union. There's a train for El Paso in about fifty-five minutes. If we move fast we can find a doctor, get the slug out of him, patch him up, and be on our way.''

A knock at the door. It startled all three. It sounded to Raider like the thud of a coffin hitting the bottom of a grave.

"This is Sheriff Cudahy. Open up.''

Doc froze Thatcher with a quick glare. Raider's eyes were on him like two muzzles preparing to fire.

"You keep your mouth shut," hissed Doc. "One word and you stay here and hang. You're an accomplice to murder."

"Open up."

"Right away, Sheriff," sang Doc, running to the door and unlocking it.

Sheriff Cudahy was a big, older man, almost seventy, but slim-waisted, his stomach flat and hard-looking, his shoulders as wide as the doorway. He was handsome, but stern-looking, mused Raider, no-nonsense, speak-when-you're-spoken-to. The old lady desk clerk stood behind him, poking her head up like a turkey, trying to see over his shoulder. Goddamn prying old maid, thought Raider, nothing to do but mind other folks' business.

Cudahy came in. She followed. He turned to her, smiling graciously.

"Thank you, Miss Dileone."

"Can't I stay?"

"Hadn't you better get back down to your desk? You shouldn't be leaving it unattended."

"It's all right, just for a few minutes." She discovered Thatcher, lifted her bony hand, and pointed at him. "That's the one that's hurt, and this one here brought him up. I knew something was fishy, I just felt it. Woman's intuition, you know."

"I appreciate it, always have. And everybody should be as civic-minded as you, as conscious of their community obligations, so to speak. But now you really should be getting back downstairs. Okay?"

She made a face of resentment, pouted, and thundered silently out. Sheriff Cudahy locked the door. His eyes drifted from Doc to Raider to Thatcher. Eyes like steel-jacketed .45s, thought Raider wearily.

"Two men have been killed and this one hurt. My instincts tell me they're all three connected." He studied Thatcher. "Tell me, laddy buck, am I right?"

"Sheriff," began Doc.

"I'm speaking to him." He crossed to where Thatcher was

sitting and stood over him, overpowering him with his size. "Who shot you, laddy buck?"

Thatcher hesitated, then nodded toward Raider.

"I shot him, all right, and killed his sidekick. He killed our prisoner in cold blood."

"Prisoner?"

"An actor by the name of Chad Bolton," explained Doc. He produced his wallet, holding up his I.D. card. "My partner and I are Pinkertons." Raider showed his card.

Cudahy examined one, then the other. "Weatherbee and Raider." His eyes narrowed. "Do I know you two? Have we met before?"

Doc shook his head. "Not to my knowledge. We just got into town today."

"Didn't take you long to stir things up, did it? Weatherbee and Raider. Raider and Weatherbee." His glance was drifting about the room. It lit on the newspaper earlier tossed into the corner. He walked over and picked it up.

"Pinkertons. Weatherbee. Raider. Here we are. . . . Weatherbury? Raynor?"

"They misspelled our names," said Doc evenly.

"That's not very charitable of them. It says here some people suspect you're in on the kidnapping of your chief."

"Speculative nonsense," said Doc. "Half an hour ago I sent a wire to the office superintendent in Chicago informing him of our progress in our search for Chief Pinkerton. If you don't believe me, check with the clerk at Western Union."

"I believe you. This article doesn't say the Pinkerton Agency suspects you." He looked at Raider. "You, laddy buck, want to tell me about it?"

Raider explained, glancing at Doc every so often, asking corroboration with his eyes. Doc obliged, nodding, nodding. . . .

"So that's how it all happened," said Cudahy. His voice was surprisingly mild. He seemed the sort who never got riled, never let loose the reins of his temper. Couldn't be bothered to. His strongest suit was his appearance: commanding, authoritative. He obviously made it work for him. It was working now.

He bent over Thatcher and examined his wound. "Hurt?"

"Fierce. It's killin' me. The mortification's settin' in."

"Jesus Christ!" bellowed Raider. "You say that word one more time . . ."

"Easy, easy," said Cudahy, without raising his voice. "The man's in pain, he's worried about his future. We'll get you to a doctor, laddy buck, just relax."

"We were hoping to leave town on the next train," began Doc.

Cudahy shrugged. "So?"

"Are we free to go?"

"I don't see why not. You, laddy, I'd like a statement from before you leave."

Raider nodded. "We have to take him along," he said. "With Bolton out o' the picture he's our only hope o' locatin' the chief."

"You want to take him down to Mexico? Oh my, I'm afraid not. He's not going anyplace."

"After his wound's treated," said Doc.

"Not even then. He's all I've got, apart from your partner's statement. Material witness. Even better, accomplice to murder."

"Sheriff, you don't understand," said Raider. "Without him to show us where they're holdin' the chief, we're licked."

"Could be. I see what you mean. Sorry."

Raider could see that Doc was beginning to lose patience. The telltall indications were always the same: the frown, clenched teeth, breathing in and holding it for a time, fidgeting.

"Sheriff," said Doc. "Clancy is holding Allan Pinkerton hostage. You saw the paper. If Governor Garber doesn't release Clancy's sons, Allan Pinkerton dies."

Cudahy nodded. "That would be a pity. I mean that sincerely."

"More than a pity, much more to us. To a lot of people, including his wife and family. The governor's on record as refusing to call off the executions. He's being adamant."

"You think he's wrong?"

"It's not a question of right or wrong, not that clear-cut, not from our point of view. As we see it, he's playing with Allan Pinkerton's life."

"You think he should let all six Clancy boys go. Then their father will release Mr. Pinkerton unharmed. Laddy buck, I'm afraid you don't see the principle involved. Or don't want to. Think about it: If every governor caved in to threats like this one, every police chief, sheriff, every authority, the entire system of law enforcement could conceivably collapse overnight. You see *that*, don't you?"

"Don't patronize me," rasped Doc. "I don't appreciate it. We need this man. He'll be returned to your custody after he's served his purpose. You have our word as agency operatives. We'll put it in writing."

"I don't want it. I don't need it. This boy's not going anywhere, except with me. On your feet, laddy buck. I'm taking you over to St. Vincent's Hospital. Dr. Holzknecht'll fix you up good as new."

"Sheriff . . ." Doc started toward him, and stopped.

Cudahy turned to Raider. "Remember to write out your statement before you leave town. Drop it off at the desk. One of my boys'll pick it up later. Pleasure meeting you two. Good hunting. I hope you get your chief back. I mean it, sincerely."

He left, Thatcher preceding him out.

CHAPTER TWELVE

No sooner had the sound of their footsteps faded into silence then Doc picked up a chair, lifted it high, and hurled it against the wall, smashing two of the legs and loosening a slat that fell on end, tipped over, and rattled to rest. Raider gaped. In all the years of their association, in the midst of all Doc's most memorable outbursts of anger, he had never seen him do such a thing, anything like it.

He laid a placating hand on his shoulder. "Doc . . ."

Doc pushed it off. "Lay off."

"Look at the bright side. We know old man Clancy is somewhere down near Rosales. That's a big help. At least we're not gonna have to range all over Chihuahua."

Doc stiffened and held his hand up, commanding silence. To Raider's astonishment a smile slowly developed, brightening his face.

"What?" asked Raider.

"We'll go over his head. To the governor. We'll lay it all on his desk. He'll understand. He'll talk to Cudahy, Mr. Laddy Buck. We'll get Thatcher back, and when we get the chief back we'll bring Thatcher back here. Think about it, Rade, all we'll really be doing is borrowing him."

"Like back home when you borrow your neighbor's best hound to go out after a razorback."

"The same."

Republican Party bigwigs in Washington considered the post of territorial governor of distant New Mexico of little importance. They had advised President Hayes to give the job to General Lew Wallace, arguing that it wouldn't look like a plum, but merely one more assignment for a man with a long record of service to his country. Wallace was dispatched to Santa Fe.

He was fifty-one years old. Earlier, at the beginning of the Civil War, he had become commanding officer of the Eleventh Indiana Infantry. He served in the West Virginia campaign with distinction, and in September 1861 was appointed brigadier-general. His greatest triumphs lay ahead of him. He fought at Shiloh in 1862 as a major-general and later commanded the Eighth Corps headquartered in Baltimore. By delaying the Confederate general, J. A. Early, at Monocacy in July 1864, he saved Washington from almost certain capture. Overnight he became a national hero.

Apart from his military exploits, he was a painter and a writer of no mean abilities. His novel *The Fair God*, published in 1873, had earned him recognition in literary circles.

Raider and Doc found him a tall, slender, dark-haired man with a full beard and dark, penetrating eyes—features somewhat suggestive of Abraham Lincoln's, only much handsomer.

His office in the palace was lined floor to ceiling with bookshelves, with only the windows and an occasional patch of wall, on which one of his paintings hung, interrupting the stacked parade of titles. Doc's impression as they entered was that the governor had deliberately walled himself off from the outside world with books. No more courtroom battles as a youthful lawyer, no more bloody battles as a war hero. Only the peace and quiet and the problem-free life of a territorial governor. Peaceful, quiet, and problem-free up until one hour ago.

Governor Wallace sat at his desk, reading. As they approached, he closed his book, rose to his feet, and showed them the title: *Buffalo Bill, the King of the Border Men*. Doc tried to suppress a grin. The governor smiled.

"Yes, Ned Buntline's best, and very good, too. Exciting. Did you know that he once wrote a novel over six hundred pages long in only sixty-two hours? It takes me months and months. You're Pinkerton agents. . . ."

Doc introduced them.

"What seems to be the problem?" the governor asked.

Doc explained. The further he got into recounting their meeting with Sheriff Cudahy, the deeper became the furrows in Wallace's forehead. He sat slouched in his chair, his fingers clasped over the Phi Beta Kappa key on his watch chain.

"I haven't talked with the sheriff," he said. "I just heard about the shootings not ten minutes ago. I'll accept your version of what happened. I did read about Chief Pinkerton's abduction."

"Governor," said Doc, "I'll be blunt. We very much want to 'borrow' Thatcher."

"You obviously need him. The problem is, Leland Cudahy won't let you have him."

"We know you're busy, sir," began Raider.

The governor chuckled and held up the Buntline book. "Positively overwhelmed with the burdens of office. I presume you want me to talk to the sheriff. I wish I could, but I'm afraid it's out of the question. Let me explain. Sheriff Cudahy is the law in Santa Fe County. It's his jurisdiction; he's responsible for keeping order. He does an excellent job. What you're asking me to do is overrule him, substitute my judgment for his in this matter." He shook his head. "That doesn't seem right, fair. Does it to either of you?"

"Allan Pinkerton's life is at stake," Doc said. "With all due respect, there's nothing right or fair about that."

"Agreed. That's the unfortunate part. But you can be sure the sheriff's taken that into consideration. You two don't know Leland. He's not being obstinate, not in the least. On the contrary, he's an intelligent man and he keeps his mind open. But he *is* conscientious, and extremely sensitive regarding his authority—the parameters of his power, so to speak. Like every other sheriff, he's elected by popular vote. It would severely damage his image if I were to ignore his decision in this matter, if I ordered him to give this man Thatcher back to you. I know you need him, desperately. I know what's at stake. But . . ."

He spread his hands, gesturing helplessness.

There was a long, weighty silence. The walls of books seemed to move inward.

"I understand," said Doc at last. "I just wonder if Mrs. Pinkerton will if her husband dies."

Raider winced, but the governor's expression did not alter in the least. His eyes showed no annoyance. Instead, anxiety appeared to be setting in. Was the problem beginning to gnaw? Perhaps, but not enough to change his mind. Raider's own mind advised that Wallace's was made up. There was nothing to be gained by pressing the man. Before the war he had been a lawyer; it was through a lawyer's eyes that he saw this situation. It obviously was the only way he *could* see it.

"If I were to go along with you," said Wallace, "if I asked, not ordered, mind you, just requested Leland as a personal favor to turn him over to you, he would do so. He wouldn't like it, but he'd comply. Then off you two'd go, leaving him here with two dead men, stripped of the accomplice, his case literally snatched from his hands, and with it, his authority. I've talked enough about that. I know Leland Cudahy. I know he's not kicking his heels and howling over this thing. To him it's all in a day's work. He doesn't need the publicity, doesn't want it. But something else he doesn't want is the governor cropping his sword."

The interview was over. They thanked Wallace and left.

Outside in the plaza it was starting to get dark. Doc paused to light an Old Virginia cheroot. He drew on it, contemplating the developing ash, mulling over the situation.

"I hate to say it, Doc," said Raider, "but you blew it. We never should have gone to him. You threw that blue fit up in the room, and the chair, and the first thing popped into your head was run to him. What we shoulda done was find us a judge, get a court order, make Cudahy hand over Thatcher."

"Rade, whether you want to believe it or not, we just talked to the judge."

"What's that supposed to mean?"

"Governor Wallace obviously knows Cudahy. Any judge in the area knows him just as well. They wouldn't step on the man's pride for a couple of strangers either. Cudahy's an intriguing sort. He's two cuts above your run-of-the-mill peace officer. He's bright, knows his job, does it well. If the governor holds him in high esteem, everybody else in authority must also. I didn't 'blow' anything. I tried and it didn't work, it couldn't.'' He paused and smoked, then resumed. ''Didn't Cudahy ask you for a statement? Let's go back to the hotel. You can get pen and ink from our dear friend Miss Dileone.''

''To hell with her! Goddamn busybody! If she'd minded her own business we'd be on the train to El Paso now. With Thatcher. We'da never even crossed trails with Cudahy.''

''Let's go see him.''

''What the hell for? He's already turned us down flat.''

Darkness was coming on rapidly, the soft, gray light of evening draining from the sky. The air was still over the city and remarkably clear. To the north the Sangre de Cristo range, the southern reach of the Rockies, stood sharply outlined against the deepening blackness. Sounds reached their ears with startling clarity: a guitar being strummed, a woman's laughter, the mingling conversations of people seated at tables in an open-air restaurant at the far corner of the plaza, barely visible through the boughs of the cottonwood trees surrounding the bandstand.

''Let's give it one more try,'' said Doc, smiling. ''Who knows? Since we last talked he may have thought about it.''

''Doc, we need that guy. He's our hound dog. He can run old man Clancy up a tree for us. Without him we're dead.''

''Let's go.''

Cudahy was in his office, sitting reading the paper, his feet up on his desk. He looked like a man without a care weightier than the decision as to what to order for supper. The office was tidy, frugally furnished, one extra chair only. The stocks of the four Remingtons in the wall rack were polished to a shine. The flat-topped desk was devoid of clutter. There was an in-out box, a small calendar tacked to the wall over it, and the wastebasket under the desk was empty. Even the keys on the ring on the peg alongside the rifle rack were in perfect alignment. Orderliness in thought, in action, in everything seemed to be Leland Cudahy's passion. Lowering his feet, he folded the paper.

"Hello again, Doc, Raider." He shook their hands. "I just got back from St. Vincent's with our friend. He's all patched up." He grinned. "I think we caught it before the 'mortification.' He's going to live." He jerked a thumb over his shoulder. "He's back in number four. I see you boys paid your respects to the governor. I wasn't spying," he added hastily. "Just happened to see you coming out of the palace as I was coming in with Thatcher."

"We asked him to, ah . . ." Doc hesitated.

"Ask me to let you have Thatcher. You don't have to tell me how it went. It's no business of mine. Raider, have you got that statement for me?"

"Give me pencil and paper and I'll write it out."

"Sure thing."

Cudahy supplied him with the essentials, pulling the extra chair up to the side of his desk.

"Sorry we're a little short of seating around here," he said to Doc. He winked. "Actually, there's a reason. It discourages loitering. There are fellows in this town with nothing to do all day long. They'd love to sit around here gossiping."

Raider licked the end of the pencil and continued writing.

"The two bodies are over at Hellman and Shaker's Funeral Parlor. I'll be dropping by there in an hour or so. By that time Tom—Tom Shaker, that is—will be through working." He glanced at Raider, who finished writing and pushed the statement and the pencil toward him. "I'm sure what he finds in his examination will tally with what you told me. Let's have a look here. Pretty short, isn't it?"

"It all happened pretty fast," said Raider. "Bolton set his bags down smack in the middle of the cross street. That was his big mistake. It gave the tall one, Jephtha, time to spot him. Then when Bolton walked on, out he came and let him have it."

"Jephtha?"

"I got that from Thatcher. He can tell you his last name."

"Tom Shaker should have his wallet. I appreciate this, Raider. You boys plan to catch the next train down to Lamy? I don't know the schedule. Would you believe I haven't been out of this town on a train in almost four years?"

"Sheriff," said Doc, "we need Thatcher. He's indispensable to our investigation. Can't you possibly see your way clear to release him into our custody? We'll return him. It may be a week, even two, but we'll be back here with him and hand him over."

Cudahy scratched his head and looked down at his drawn-together knees. He was turning Doc's words over as if, thought Raider, staring at him, to examine the underside, like a steak on a brazier.

"I've thought about it since we talked. There's one way." The two Pinkertons tensed expectantly, Raider leaning forward in his chair. "I can let you have him, Doc, only it'll have to be a quid pro quo. I keep Raider here in his place."

"Oh for Chrissakes," began Raider.

"Can I finish? I have two men dead, shot down in the street. The law says I have every right to hold both Raider and Thatcher, but I understand what you two are up against so I'm willing to let you leave town." His eyes shifted to Raider, then back to Doc. "But if I let Thatcher go too, all I'm left with is this statement."

Raider exhaled in exasperation. "It's all you need."

"I disagree. It may be all over for you two, but I still have work to do. I have to get Dr. Holzknecht and Tom Shaker, the undertaker, together and get a written report on each one of the bodies: the wounds, points of entry of the slugs in both cases, estimated distances—all the little details. Then I ring in Judge Wiles. There won't be a formal inquest, of course, but the judge has to be filled in on every aspect of the thing."

"Come on, Sheriff," said Raider, "that's horse water and you know it! You got yourself four planks and you're trying to build a damn barn. We're talkin' here about a cut-and-dried street gun-down. You got all the facts right there written down."

"Raider, are you trying to tell me my job?"

"No, no," said Doc hastily. "Not for a minute. The law's the law, and nobody respects it more than the agency, meaning Pinkerton operatives. You'll do what you have to, of course. But Thatcher—"

"Is an accessory to murder," said Cudahy evenly. "An accomplice."

"The bastard was unarmed," sputtered Raider hotly.

"Sheriff," said Doc, "you say accessory to murder, accomplice, but think about that. Is he really? What is an accomplice, actually?"

"One associated with the guilty party in the commission of a crime."

"Whether he's the principal or an accessory, he's a participant in a crime."

"Precisely."

"Okay," Doc went on. "There's no disputing the fact that Thatcher was present, that he was with Jephtha Whatever-his-name-was. But as Rade says, Thatcher was unarmed."

"I made him turn out his pockets. He didn't even have a penknife on him."

Doc stopped him with a gesture. "Accessory, accomplice. If a man opens the door of a bank and his friends go in and loot it, that man is an accomplice. If a man merely holds the reins of the others' horses while they commit the crime, he too is an accomplice. But Thatcher's only connection with these shootings, something all three of us agree on, is that *he was with Jephtha*. He didn't hand him the gun, didn't hold his horse, didn't point out Bolton for him . . ."

"Wait, wait, wait," said Cudahy smiling. "Now, you've hit it. You say he *didn't* point out Bolton. How do you know that? How do you know he wasn't along for precisely that reason: to identify Bolton. *Because he knew what he looked like and Jephtha didn't.*"

Raider felt his heart cave in like a floor buckling under too much weight. Cudahy's intelligence was just too heavy for the floor of Doc's argument. The man was right. He, Raider, should know. In his shirt pocket was the newspaper picture of

Chad Bolton that Thatcher had reluctantly handed over when he'd asked him to turn out his pockets. It appeared that the only reason why Thatcher had come up from Mexico with Jephtha was to locate Bolton and *point him out*. They knew he was being held; they knew the Pinkertons would be on their way down to Mexico to try to rescue the chief; they knew they'd be taking the fastest way south, the A.T.&S.F.

Nevertheless, Doc refused to accept defeat. "Has Thatcher admitted that?"

Cudahy smirked. "Would you if you were he? Dumb as he is, and he's dumb, he's not about to volunteer information— certainly not anything that could hang him. Laddy buck, you're grasping at straws."

"The man's right," said Raider dejectedly. Doc glared at him.

"All right, all right, all right! You win, Sheriff, but would you do this much? Would you at least let us have a word with him?"

"By all means."

Cudahy got up, got down the key ring, and gestured for them to follow him. A thought impinged itself on Raider's mind. Granted, Cudahy was right, Thatcher had fingered Bolton for Jephtha, but why send Jephtha up to do the job? Why couldn't Thatcher do it? Why two men to do a one-man job?

Could be Thatcher couldn't pull a trigger. Some can't, can't even shoot a javelina after it's stunk up their bedroll. He'd met a few in his time, men who couldn't be peace officers and couldn't ride the outlaw trail either. They became clerks or preachers, book writers or schoolteachers, any job of work that a gun didn't go with. . . .

Thatcher had his shirt off. A descending spica bandage covered his shoulder and his wound. Cudahy left Raider and Doc standing outside the cell, considerably closing the inner door to afford them privacy.

"How you feeling?" Raider asked solicitously.

"Lousy. Doc give me something for the pain, but it still hurts like hell," whined Thatcher. He glared at Raider. "Thanks a heap."

"Now, wait a minute. You boys shot our man, you ran away, what else could I do but chase after you, fetch you back? Don't go blaming these bars on us. We didn't call in the sheriff. You want to blame somebody, how about that old maid desk clerk?"

"It was still you that shot me, give me all this pain. Now they're fixin' to string me up for bein' 'complice. I ain't no such a thing. I wasn't even wearin' iron."

"We know all that," said Doc impatiently.

"What do you want with me now?" Thatcher looked from one to the other suspiciously.

"Nothing big," said Raider. "Just a couple fast answers. Where exactly is old man Clancy? I know you said down around Rosales, but where? In a house? A damn cave? Where? What does it look like? What are the trail signs? Is there any kinda road leadin' up to the place?"

"Why in hell should I tell you? Anythin'. Why should I give you spit on your boot?"

Raider bristled. "On account if that old maid hadn't stuck her big nose into this business, we'd all three be on the train to El Paso now."

"And what'd be so great about that? We get down there and old leather face'd spot us comin' and start shootin' up a storm. Right off he'd cut me in half. What's the difference 'tween a rope an' a shotgun. Dead is dead, ain't that so?"

"You're not going to hang," said Raider mildly, striving for reassurance in his tone.

"The hell I ain't, I'm 'complice."

"You're not, goddamn it! The worst they'll give you is ninety days in the big pasture, makin' hair bridles. Good eats, plenty o' sleep."

"How do you know how long they'll give me? I could get ten years easy. I could swing. God Almighty, Almighty, Almighty . . ."

"Just answer the question," said Raider sternly, "or I'll goddamn guarantee you swing!" He fished in his pocket, at the same time glancing at the closed door. He lowered his voice. "You recollect this?" He held up Bolton's picture.

"You were carryin' it. You spotted him, pointed him out to your partner. Now, listen, Artis Henry. We didn't show this to Sheriff Cudahy. You know that's a fact. If we did he'da taken it for evidence, right?"

Thatcher nodded slowly.

Raider waved the picture. "Us keeping this proves we're tryin' real hard to play square with you. But if you don't give us the answers we want, I'll shove this down Cudahy's throat. It'll be all he needs to come down on you like an anvil."

Like a snake striking, Thatcher's hand shot out between the bars, snatching the picture. Into his mouth it went. He began chewing, grinning his crooked grin, chewing, swallowing. Raider cursed and threw himself hard against the bars, reaching in, stretching his arm, his fingers working futilely. Thatcher stepped back.

"By God, that tasted mighty fine. Sweet as a honeycake."

"You little bastard!"

Doc threw up his hands and turned his back on them, his shoulders slumping discouragedly.

"Come on, Rade, let's get out of here."

"Like hell! You listen to me, Thatcher. I'll give you one last chance. Where's Clancy hiding out? How many men with him? Come on, tell us."

"Go find yourself a mule's asshole an' ask it, Pink. I ain't tellin' you nothin'. You'll never find old leather face or your boss. You can run yourselves ragged all over Mexico with seven hundred guns, with the Texas Rangers, the U.S. Army, you won't find shit!" He started to laugh.

Again Raider threw himself at the bars. Again Thatcher backed off, continuing to laugh, pointing, slapping his knee, laughing, laughing.

They left. Outside in the plaza Doc lit another Old Virginia. "Congratulations," he said icily.

"What's biting you?"

" 'Shove this down Cudahy's throat.' You had to say it, didn't you? Had to put it in just those words." He faced him, scowling. "Had to put the idea in his head. Why didn't you do it up brown, ask Cudahy for a plate and a fork? He could have boiled it and given it to him for supper.''

"Why don't you shut your big mouth!''

Doc shook his head and obliged. They walked in silence toward the hotel, passing a street band playing spiritedly, the happy faces of the musicians and of those watching and listening as bright as the street lanterns overhead. Doc hurried his pace, leaving Raider two, then three steps behind.

Raider made no effort to catch up.

CHAPTER THIRTEEN

The searching, conquering and destroying conquistadores arrived in present-day El Paso four centuries ago. The city is situated at the lowest natural pass between Mexico and the United States, where the westernmost tip of Texas touches Mexico and New Mexico. To the north the bare, craggy peaks of the Franklin Mountains climb 7,000 feet. To the east lay arid plains interrupted only by flat desert tablelands. South and west, the Sierra Madre begins, buckling the surface of the earth in twin chains stretching all the way down to the Gulf of Tehuantepec.

The population of the town Raider and Doc arrived in had more than doubled in the past two months, following the arrival of the railroad. Bankers, merchants, real-estate brokers, cattlemen, miners, railroad men, gamblers, saloon keepers, and men and women seeking work of any sort—and with it a new beginning for their lackluster lives and failed ambitions—had flocked in. They had come by rail; in hacks, buggies, and wagons; on horseback; and even afoot. El Paso's four small hotels were crammed to the ridge poles; people paid to sleep in the lobbies. El Paso Street, the main thoroughfare, was so crowded at all hours that pedestrian traffic overflowed the sidewalks. Nearly every corner boasted a saloon with an attached gambling house. Two variety theaters, the Coliseum, operated by the Manning brothers, and Jack Doyle's, played to capacity audiences at every performance—good, bad, or atrocious.

Raider had had his fill of riding trains long before they reached Santa Fe. By the time they arrived in El Paso, the iron horse had chugged to the top of his hate list. He could walk, he could sit a saddle . . .

"But on a damn train seat a man's got no place for his legs. Legs should hang, not just stand in front o' you like two posts. My ass is so flat it's crumpled my backbone!"

"Quit complaining," said Doc. "How do you think mine feels?"

They stood at the corner of El Paso Street and Magoffen, the crowd surging around them, occasionally jostling, setting Raider glaring.

"If we don't start getting lucky pretty soon," went on Doc, "that may be the last train you'll ever ride on."

"Goddamn Cudahy, laddy buck bastard! We could be in great shape now if it wasn't for him."

"I've been thinking about him, Rade, and Governor Wallace. You know what the problem is?"

"Hell, yes!"

"I don't mean their not letting us take custody of Thatcher. I mean why they both seem to take the chief's situation so lightly. It's because neither believes Governor Garber will go through with the executions. Not the way things stand. Allan Pinkerton has too many friends in high places. General McClellan is now governor of New Jersey; he could be sitting in the White House some day."

"Abe Lincoln beat his pants off in sixty-four."

"Just the same, he's an important man, and a close friend. President Grant, Chief Justice Waite, Commodore Vanderbilt—they're all close friends. You'd think they'd turn their backs on him?"

"It's not up to them, it's up to that governor."

"Garber."

"You read the Santa Fe paper. He says he's not about to knuckle under."

"I know what it *said*."

"He could be one stubborn son of a bitch. We don't know."

"Let's get a newspaper, see if there're any new developments."

"Let's not. Things are bad enough already. I don't want to know anything that's gonna make 'em worse."

His objection was ignored. They wedged through the crowd and crossed the street to a variety store. Doc bought a copy of the weekly El Paso *Sun* from a boy at the stand outside. The date under the headline indicated it had just come out that day. There was nothing about either the kidnapping or the Clancys on the front page.

"Doc, isn't there anything in that report Wagner give you in Chicago, the three pages on the Clancys out of the file?"

Doc leafed through the paper. "Come on, you know yourself file reports are about as useful as an extra great toe. They're usually dated and always vague: heights, weights, ages, past histories. There's nothing that's going to help us at this stage."

"Just the same, maybe you should dig it outta your bag and let's have another look."

"Hold it, here's something."

"What?"

"Sssssh. Oh, my God!"

"I knew it! I knew it! I told you not to buy the damn thing."

"Garber's announced that he's proceeding with the executions. They're scheduled for Monday the twelfth."

"That only gives us ten days. That's crazy! It'll take at least three weeks to get down to Rosales, let alone locate where they're at. It's gotta be close to three hundred miles easy."

Doc closed the paper. A passer-by bumped against him, pushing him against Raider, and walked on. Doc didn't even turn to look at him; he had suddenly plunged deep into thought. There was a long silence between the two, an island of quiet in the hubbub surrounding them.

"What are we gonna do, Doc?"

"Go on as planned. What else can we do? Let's get started shopping: horses, gear, everything we'll need."

"Couple o' rifles, for sure."

"When we're done we'll go back to the railroad station and

get our things, pick out what we'll need to take with us, and store the rest.'' He folded the paper, started forward, and stopped, snapping his fingers. ''The first thing we'll need is a Spanish phrase book.''

''You mean Mex-Spanish; it's different than the real thing. I know some.''

''Sure, *dinero, señor, plaza,*—how many, thirty words? And what I know goes all the way back to prep school. It could come in handy, Rade.''

''But we won't be hittin' towns the way we're heading. It's gonna be burro and barefoot country all the way, rurals. They're not Spanish-type Mexicans, they're Indians. Their ancestors were there long before the Spanish come.''

''We're going to end up in Rosales, hopefully. We'll need a phrase book.'' He stared at Raider. ''It's going to be a hard ride, isn't it?''

''I guess. It'll be infuriatin' slow, 'specially when we get into the hills; up and down, up and down. We should buy horses *and* burros.''

The little store was crammed with people. Take away the clerks and the merchandise and one would have imagined it a railroad station with the entire town impatiently waiting for the last train out, mused Doc. They pushed toward the counter. Finally they got up to it and waited their turn to talk to a man with fire-red hair so thick, top and sides, it dwarfed his face. He looked harried, overworked, and resentful because of it.

''What, what, what?''

''Do you have a Spanish-English phrase book?'' Doc asked.

The man reached under the counter and slapped down a book. The cover displayed crossed American and Mexican flags. Doc began leafing through it.

''Mister, this ain't no liberry. You want it or don'tcha?''

''Yes.''

''Twenty-five cents.''

''Do you have any maps of Mexico? Chihuahua, perhaps?''

''Nope. Twenty-five cents.''

''No Chihuahua, or no maps whatsoever?''

''Whatsoever. Twenty-five cents.''

"Amazing."

"Yeah. Twenty-five cents!"

"Hey, Doc, look."

Behind the man racks filled with five-cent pulp magazines climbed to the low ceiling: *Buffalo Bill Stories, The Wide Awake Library, The Half Dime Reading Library, The Brave and Bold, Work and Win,* and dozens of others. But it wasn't the novels that had caught Raider's eye, it was the current issue of *Frank Leslie's Illustrated Newspaper.* Filling the front page was an artist's rendering of a familiar face. Above it, one word: "Missing."

"The chief!" exclaimed Doc. "Give us that *Leslie's,* too," he said to the man.

"Fifteen cents."

"It says ten right on it," interposed Raider.

"We get fifteen for it, take it or leave it. Forty cents in all," added the man to Doc.

They stood outside, their backs flat against the window, avoiding the passing crowd. Doc ran through the article.

"There's nothing here we don't know already, except that everybody's looking for him up around Cheyenne."

"How dumb can they get!" sputtered Raider. "The Chicago office knows old man Clancy's in Mexico, for Chrissakes."

"According to this, the Chicago office isn't talking. Not a whisper. No, there's nothing new here."

"Give it here. I'll take it back and get our money back."

"You can't do that. I'll toss it in the next trash barrel. Only we should keep the picture. It's a good likeness. Excellent. Taken from a photograph. When we get to where we're going we can show it around."

"I don't know, Doc. You show it to the wrong fella and off he'll run to Clancy and spill the beans we're there. Some o' those peons'd peddle their soul for six pesos or a jug o' pulque. The one thing, maybe the only thing we got in our favor is the element o' surprise."

"We don't have that. Clancy knows we're going to show up sooner or later."

"Goddamn Artis Henry Thatcher! The least he coulda done

was tell us how many guns they got down there. We could wind up facing twenty or thirty men!''

"We'll know when we get there. Let's go buy us some transportation.''

Raider suggested that they buy their saddles first, complaining as he did so that he'd "left the best damn saddle in the world in storage back at the agency.'' They found a saddler at the corner of Santa Fe Street within sight of the bridge across the Rio Grande. The place was in awesome disarray, saddles lying about the floor and piled one on top of another: westerns, Californias, Texas saddles, Denvers, most of them used, many in horrendous condition, leather torn, pommels broken, stirrups worn nearly through, rivets missing. The man in charge was ancient, bewhiskered, stumpy, outrageously bowlegged, and smelled of stale liquor. His eyes betrayed his activity of the night before. They were as red as unripe cherries.

"We're lookin' for a couple westerns," said Raider. "Used, but not too.'' He pointed at one, then another western saddle atop a pile. "Not ruined and useless like that junk.''

"That 'junk' happens to be two fine E. L. Gallatins—best in the West.''

"They maybe were, but neither one's got four miles ridin' left in it.''

"You think you know saddles, pilgrim?''

"I know a good one when I see it.'' Raider looked around. "Finding one here's like lookin' for a needle in the hay.''

The old man bristled. "You want quality, you want craftsmanship, you come looky here.'' He walked them into a corner and, bending, began pulling saddles out of a pile, building another pile alongside. He stopped pulling when he came to three used westerns. Used, but in good condition. Doc pulled Raider to one side.

"We should buy new ones. We can afford it,'' he whispered.

"No way. I don't fancy breaking in a new saddle on the trek we got ahead of us. I'll handle this.''

He crouched and examined one, then another saddle.

"These two are okay, I guess.''

"Okay? Pilgrim, they're good as new. Better, they're broke in. They're great quality. You got eyes, you can see. An' best of all, the price is a steal. Only forty bucks."

Doc reacted in silent surprise. Raider did not—didn't even blink, and didn't raise his voice.

"New, thirty. Used, half price. Fifteen."

The old man gasped, reacting as if Raider had slapped his face.

"Pilgrim, I ain't hearin' right."

"Fifteen bucks!"

"Pilgrim, you *are* funnin' me. You got to be. Look, you see what's outside that door? El Paso. This here town's so crowded a river rat couldn't find room to lay hisself down. Look at that street. Ever see so much humanity in your life? You know what a overcrowded town means? It means a seller's market, that's what. Pilgrim, I could get fifty bucks apiece for these here seats."

Raider turned and started off. "Go get it. Come on, Doc."

"Wait, wait! Listen to me. I like you boys. Liked you the minute I laid eyes on you, comin' through the door. You boys Baptists?"

"Fifteen bucks," said Raider.

"Twenny-five."

"Sixteen."

"Oh, for God sakes. I come down a whole five an' you only go up a stinkin' dollar? That ain't fair."

"Twenty dollars," said Doc.

Raider glared. Doc shut him up, squeezing his forearm.

"Twenty-four," said the man.

They bought both saddles for forty-five dollars. They also bought split-ear headstalls and curbs. The old man, irritated, muttering in his unkempt whiskers as he took their money and they walked out, barked a response to Doc's question.

"Orson Maltby's Livery Stable. On Magoffin. You'll see the sign, iffn you can read."

Out they walked, their saddles on their shoulders. Doc turned to look back. He chuckled. The old man was smiling proudly to himself. Raider saw him.

"Twenty-two fifty is about four-fifty too much," he said. "If you'da let me do the talkin', I'da got him down to seventeen, eighteen-fifty."

Compared to the saddler's shop, Orson Maltby's Livery Stable looked as neat and orderly as Sheriff Cudahy's office. Maltby wasn't in; his father greeted them, introducing himself. He was at least ten years older than the saddler, well into his eighties, beardless, his face deeply lined and wrinkled as a prune. And his complexion very nearly as dark. Curiously, his eyes looked like they belonged in the face of one fifty years younger; they were light blue and twinkled, lighting up his smile.

He had more than thirty horses to choose from. They were corralled out back, milling about, the stallions whinnying, the mares quiet as usual. Here was some good-looking horseflesh, mused Raider, for sale at top dollar, no doubt. The saddler was right; the town had to be a seller's market. Money was no problem to them; they still had well over $2,000 of Bolton's blood money. But, Raider thought, he'd be damned if he'd give it away or see Doc give it away to these money-hungry border thieves. Forty dollars was a high price for a good horse anywhere in the territories; anything over would be road agent robbery.

He spied a small bay with a mean look in his eye, tough-looking, able to take the mountains and desert with ease, probably, but also probably stubborn as a mule. You could tell a lot from a horse's eyes; he could. Here was one you could get fifty miles out of one day, and four the next. A horse with a mind of its own was no buy at any price.

"You like that bay?" Maltby asked.

"Maybe. Looks a little ornery."

"Might I ask where you boys are heading?"

"No place special," said Raider hurriedly, looking warningly at Doc who had opened his mouth to answer and now closed it.

"I mean to say if you're heading south you'll need good strong mounts, good wind, good endurance. And if you're going into cow work the same holds true."

Doc pointed out a big-boned, thickset pinto with a bald face. "That pinto."

"Good horse, strong as a bull. He could take you over the Rockies without raising a sweat. Look at that barrel, those legs. Good all-around horse."

"How much?" asked Raider.

"Same price for every horse. Sixty dollars."

"That's pretty steep."

"My son Orson sets the price. These horses are all broken, all ready to ride. He pays double to break a horse, ten dollars per. Everybody else only pays five, but we want ours properly broken. Thoroughly. Some fellows take three or four days. There's not a horse in here that hasn't had a full week of breaking. Ride any one of them, you'll see."

"We believe you," said Doc, feeling Raider's eyes on him.

Raider grunted. "Sixty bucks is still steep. We've been all over, even California. I never seen a horse priced higher than thirty-five."

"We'll pay your price," said Doc evenly.

"The hell you say!" burst Raider.

"On condition you let us try them. A good run up the line and back."

"That's fair, but you'll have to give me cash."

"It's a deal."

He and Maltby shook hands.

"Now, just a damn minute, Doc. Sixty bucks is crazy. I can buy two mounts for that in Cheyenne, Tucson, Butte, Potlach, any place you say."

"I don't doubt it," said Maltby, "but not here. Not since the railroad came in."

Raider scoffed. "It's a seller's market, we know. We been hearin' it all over town."

"I'll take the pinto," said Doc. "What do you like, Rade?"

"I don't much like sixty bucks, I can tell you that."

"Pick one out."

"Chrissakes. Okay, okay. That grey, the one with the black mane."

"You've got a good eye, mister."

"Yeah, yeah."

"I mean it. I've ridden that horse myself. I know every horse in this pen. Been in horses all my life. She's a winner. She's sure-footed, a fast walker, and strong. She'll carry you and three hundred pounds of buffalo meat like feathers."

Doc paid him. They saddled up and rode out of town at a gallop, following the river in the direction of Las Cruces. They rode for almost two miles before reining up.

"This is a good horse, Rade."

"Mmmmmm."

"What's the matter now?"

"Goddamn El Paso, that's what's the matter. It's the damnedest thievingest town I've ever seen, bar none. Everybody overcharges for everything."

"Simmer down, we're not exactly destitute."

Shading his eyes, Doc looked across the river. Recent rains had swollen it well beyond its normal capacity. It thrashed its banks like an enormous brown serpent slithering pell-mell toward its lair to the southeast. Beyond its foam-flecked back lay Mexico—not just another country, he thought, but another world. Before them stretched the Medanos de Samalyuca, a seemingly limitless rocky landscape studded with clumps of chino grama grass, prickly-pear cactus, spiky torrey yuccas, yellow paper flowers. Well beyond the range of his vision lay the mountains and the vast Bolsón de los Muertos—the Basin of the Dead.

And the desert. The mountains were not nearly as lofty as the Rockies, but just as difficult to get through. The trail twisted about, doubling back, circling peaks, running up against walls a thousand feet high, or ending at the rims of ravines a thousand feet deep, too wide to leap, impossible for them to cross, let alone the horses. And the mountain streams they would encounter would make the Rio Grande look like a fish pond on the move. Even more difficult, more forbidding would be the desert, lying there like a dying monster: The sand monster. No grass for the horses, no water for them, nothing but endless sand sculptured by the wind, barren of growth, hiding snakes and spiders, scorpions . . .

He shivered. Damn imagination!

"What are you thinking about, Doc? Pretty rough-lookin' country over there, right?"

"If Thatcher and his friend can do it . . ."

"If they did. Could be they were sittin' in Santa Fe just waiting for us to show."

"Isn't there a shorter route to Rosales, easier?"

"We could head on down to Presidio."

"How far?"

"Too far. I've thought about it, going down there, crossing over, and cuttin' through the Big Bend country, but it's way outta the way. From here to Presidio down to Rosales would add another eighty miles. And look at the river—we sure couldn't travel by boat. We wouldn't get two miles before we cracked up."

"I wish we had a buggy, a wagon. We could make the seat really comfortable."

"We'd never make it on wheels."

"The stage goes back and forth to Chihuahua."

"Doc, I'm sick to death o' seats. I purely got to have a horse under me. You'll be okay. You'll get used to your saddle real fast, you'll see."

Doc shook his head disconsolately and swept his hand to the south. "Look what we have to get through. There must be a million snakes, scorpions, tarantulas, lizards, wolves, pumas, jaguars . . ."

"No jaguars, except maybe a stray or two every fifty miles. None really till you get down where it's lots hotter."

"That's a comfort." Doc sighed resignedly. He studied the river in silence, letting it carry away his concerns. He smiled grimly. "At least this time of year water won't be a problem, except in the desert."

"No problem," responded Raider eagerly, raising his voice over Doc's last four words. "Even down to the Bolsón de los Muertos it can rain like hell. Ahhhh, hard. Pretty hard. But only for a little while. Then the sun comes right back out again.''

"Will you kindly stop being evasive? On top of everything else we'll have to contend with, are we going to have to brace for rotten weather all the way down?''

"Hell, no.''

"Liar!''

"Take it easy, Doc, you're getting yourself all worked up over nothin'. It's just another ride. We've done six times as bad and twice as far. Everything's gonna turn out roses. Let's go back. We still got to get these horses shod, buy rifles and ammunition, bedrolls, cooking stuff, the works.''

"We don't have to burden ourselves with groceries. We can buy most of what we'll need at the farms and villages along the way. We have to save on weight.''

"There aren't any farms or villages in the desert or the Bolsón. Besides, Mex food gripes my gut so fierce, you wouldn't believe it's possible. It's all peppers. Everything the bastards cook is hotter than blazes.''

"Not everything. I tell you we've got to travel as light as possible. We've got a long way. All we need is for one of the horses to give out on us!''

Raider patted his grey's neck affectionately. "You wouldn't give out, would you, little girl?''

The mare responded with a confident toss of her head. He laughed.

"Let's go back, load up, and get on our way. We can make a good twenty miles before dark. You watch—these two'll do it on their friggin' legs.''

"We'll see,'' said Doc somberly.

CHAPTER FOURTEEN

Raider's prediction did not begin to approach accuracy. Through the red tape and delays of Customs and a mile across the river, one look at the position of the sun convinced Doc that his partner's estimate of twenty miles before nightfall was more optimistic encouragement than reasonable reckoning. Their progress was noticeably slowed by the detritus of twenty-six million years of evolutionary change. It littered the land as far as they could see in every direction. Their horses picked their way carefully through the rocks and the vegetation, avoiding cactus and the flourishing thorny-branched ocotillo.

They covered three miles by Raider's calculations before reining up the first time. Looking behind them, they could see the river vanishing now and again behind rises in the surface as it wound its way to the southeast and the Gulf of Mexico. The forge of the heavens slipped below the Hatchet Mountains that ran north and south, clamping Old and New Mexico together. Riding under a glowing purple sky streaked with silver, they managed two more miles before darkness set in.

Raider made a fire while Doc hobbled the horses and gave them water. They nibbled the plentiful grass. Doc and Raider ate beans and fresh bread, half of the first of six loaves Raider had insisted they bring along. They drank Arbuckle's coffee, boiled in a newly purchased gray enamel pot with a retinned cover.

"My God, this coffee's strong!" exclaimed Doc.

His partner, sitting on his haunches on the opposite side of the fire, snickered, stopped short, stared, pointed at him, and broke into laughter.

"Look at you, if you don't beat all. You look like a Monkey Ward greenhorn for fair."

"I'm wearing the same things you are, you jackass—hat, shirt, denims, Justin boots. So yours are a different brand, but they look alike. They do to me."

"You think *we* look the same?" Again he laughed, slapped his knee, spilled his coffee, and laughed louder.

"Look around you, plowboy. This is scarcely the environment for expensive attire and accessories. I don't particularly relish wearing these things," he added icily. "I'm trying to be practical."

"You look about as comfortable as a blacksmith in a boiled shirt. On second thought, old A.P. was right. You look like a candy butcher working a Wild West show. That's what he said when he saw you in that getup on the train back when, a ways outta Omaha. Remember?" He leered, then sobered. "I know I shouldn't laugh at you, but you do look strange."

Doc stood up and examined his clothing. "What specifically looks so 'strange.' Tell me."

"It's not what you got on. It's not so much how you're wearin' it. It's more the condition. Take your shirt. It doesn't look proper on account it doesn't look worn. It should be splotched under the arms, down the front, down from the nape o' your neck with salt stains from sweating. And your Levi's. Man, they shine they're so new-lookin'. You oughta get yourself a handful o' gravel and rub 'em down, start gettin' the color outta them, get 'em lookin' like you live in 'em, like everybody does. And your hat . . ."

Doc took off his new Stetson and studied it inside and out. "It's exactly like yours, it just isn't battered and filthy like yours. It doesn't stink like yours."

"What are you talkin' about? My hat doesn't stink."

"It's rancid. How long have you been wearing it?"

"Four or five years, why?"

"I'll bet you've never had it cleaned and blocked, not once."

"Course not. You don't clean a John B., you asshole.

Shows you how much you know. Damn, you look so funny you got me laughing, made me spill my coffee.''

"You don't clean a John B.''

"You don't. Man, that's, that's sectrelig.''

"*Sac*rilege.''

"Whatever. You just don't. Put yours back on.'' Doc rolled his eyes impatiently but complied. "You see, you don't even know how to wear it. Here, let me.'' Raider stepped over the fire and, flipping his hands out as if to relax them for the task, slowly and carefully reset Doc's hat on his head.

"It's supposed to be worn at just the right jack-deuce angle over your left eye. You pull it down in front when the sun's in your eyes, down in the back to keep the rain outta your collar. But for ordinary wearin', that's perfect.''

"It doesn't feel comfortable.''

"It's right, I tell you. You'll get used to it. You want to look proper, don't you?''

"Of course. When I think of all the people we're going to be bumping into in the next three weeks, the celebrities, statesmen . . .''

"I'm serious, Doc, I'm tryin' to help you, give you the benefit o' my experience. Hey, when we were up to Chicago you never stopped jawing from the minute we set foot off the train to when we got back on, givin' me the benefit o' your—''

"All right, all right, all right.'' Doc finished his coffee. "Great God, this coffee is absolutely horrendous!''

Raider poured another cup, sipped some, and smacked his lips. "I call it real tasty.''

"Rade . . .''

"Yeah?''

"Your taste is in your clothes.''

Three days passed.

They sat at the campfire, supper finished, Doc enjoying his evening cheroot. Raider busied himself, examining the horse's hooves. The moon was in its first quarter, the stars swarming the heavens, sharper, brighter than Doc had ever seen them, so he remarked.

Raider grunted a rejoinder. "That blacksmith we went to knows his job. He gives a good fit, and he sure was right recommendin' bar shoes."

"If you say so. You know something, these mountains aren't nearly as rough as I imagined they'd be."

"These 'mountains' are hills. We only got one real mountain ahead of us, and that we circle. We should be seeing it in two or three days. First we got to cross the Basin of the Dead."

"Mmmm."

Raider came away from Doc's horse, back over to the fire, and squatted on his bedroll. "Something else on your mind?"

"Thatcher. One thing bothers me about him. Doesn't make sense."

Raider nodded knowingly. "I bet I know what you mean. That picture o' Bolton he was carrying. If he come along just to point Bolton out so his friend Jephtha could kill him, how come *he* had the picture? His havin' it must mean he needed it, right?"

"Mmmm."

"And if he needed *it,* it means he never actually saw Bolton in the flesh, leastwise not close up. Because if he did he wouldn't need his picture."

"Jephtha should have had the picture. He could have come alone. Why didn't he?"

"Right."

"Unless . . ." Doc scratched his chin and crinkled his brow in thought.

"What?"

"Well, if you think it through, there could be half a dozen reasons why Thatcher came along. We know he wasn't wearing a gun, so he didn't come to kill. It's possible he actually had seen Bolton and would recognize him, and was just carrying the picture to refresh his memory. The man wasn't exactly brilliant. He brought along the picture to make doubly sure they'd have the right man when they caught up with him. Remember, in the picture Bolton was in character: a wig, makeup . . .''

''You could still recognize that face.''

''True. There's another explanation. It's possible Clancy sent Thatcher along just for companionship. It's a long, lonely ride from Rosales up to Santa Fe.''

''I told you before, I don't believe they ever did come up. I say they were already there. Maybe even all the way up to Cheyenne. Hanging around, waiting for that phony accident. They followed us down, but didn't catch up until Santa Fe. They were ridin'; we were ridin' trains. Us gettin' delayed in Trinidad the way we did, they were able to catch up.''

''You're probably right. There's another explanation—about Thatcher, I mean. It could be he volunteered to go with Jephtha, claiming he knew what Bolton looked like. The old man believed him and let him go along. And he somehow got hold of that picture, and actually did make use of it, so to speak.''

''However they worked it, it's all history now.''

''What do you think they'll do with Thatcher? They certainly won't hang him.''

''They'll stick him away for a while. You know something? Cudahy really surprised me. I killed that Jephtha bastard and all he did was ask me for a statement.''

''It's all he needed. He knows where to find you if he needs you. Also, he knew what we were up against. So he bent a little.''

''He sure didn't bend on Artis Henry Thatcher after my daddy.''

Raider paused, looking off to the south into the blackness and the next set of mountains, their outline barely visible ahead. Doc followed his eyes.

''He's down there somewhere, Rade. We've got to find him.''

''Yeah.''

''This has to be the toughest one we've ever had, don't you think?''

"Just about. Funny, I was thinking the same thing. You think that governor up in Nebraska will stick by his guns? Go through with the hangings?"

"I doubt it. I don't think there's one chance in a hundred. He can't lose too much face postponing them. But understand something: That in no way eliminates our problem. Meaning Will Francis. It's what he *thinks* Garber will do. If he finds out the executions have been scheduled, and he has to have some way of getting news down there, come the twelfth, he could follow through on his threat."

"He'd be crazy to."

"His history doesn't suggest that he's all that sane."

"The man's not loco. He's sure thinkin' clear on this business."

"I have a feeling he's your classic hothead. Shoot first and sort things out later."

"We'll never make it by the twelfth."

"You think he has access to telegraph down there?"

"Bet on it. Rosales is small, but bigger than any other town around. It's got to be hooked up with the capital up the line."

"Mmm."

Doc tossed his cheroot into the dying fire. His stallion whinnied. He got up and went to it. There was nothing wrong. No snake. Raider conjectured that it had been bitten by a fly. He set about preparing his bedroll.

Seventh day.

As yet they had met no one. The mountains were at their backs. They were crossing the bleak, level, cracked floor of the Basin of the Dead. Like galleons of old, white clouds sailed across the azure sky above the horizon ahead. Above the fleet the clouds darkened and joined. Above their heads hovered a cloud as black as a mine shaft. Doc saw Raider looking up at it apprehensively.

"There's sure no ridin' out from under it."

"You think it'll break?"

"Any second."

The first drops landed like pebbles striking, hammering the brims of their hats. They tilted them back. Within a minute the rain was coming down ferociously, as if an unseen hand wielding a sword had sliced open the belly of the cloud. Both horses stopped, refusing to move a step further, lowering their heads, the mare pawing the ground, the stallion whinnying plaintively.

Raider and Doc had dismounted. They both stood stiffly, holding their reins, their shoulders hunched, bracing against the onslaught. Doc had never seen it rain so, in the first few seconds could not believe it. So powerful was it, so savage, so heavy thumping down upon his shoulders and back, for a moment he feared his knees would give way under him. Dimly through the deluge, he saw Raider less than five feet from him brace himself, one leg forward. Then he dropped to his knees. Doc followed his example, clutching his hat brim as he did so.

In his mind he pictured the rain as a hammer: solid steel pounding down, pounding him into the ground like a stake. It was as if the Gulf of Mexico had been poured into the cloud and released, billions of gallons coming down in minutes, striking the ground, disappearing in the cracks and holes.

It lasted no more than four minutes by his estimate. That seemed like four hours. It stopped as abruptly as it began.

"Looks like we're in for a little sprinkle," said Raider wearily, as he began squeezing the water out of his sleeves.

"My God," murmured Doc. "My God."

Ninth day.

The desert wasn't just a barren expanse of rumpled sand, as Doc had imagined it would be. It sustained life, growth: Scrub, creosote bush, yucca, mesquite, and prickly-pear cactus, which seemed to abound everywhere, save in the mountains. And there was occasional grass.

They camped that night where the grass sufficed in quantity to feed the horses. Sitting beside the fire, smoking a cheroot,

Doc studied the heavens. For some reason the stars seemed closer than on previous nights. It was colder, and the sweeping expanse of sand around them inspired him with a feeling of smallness, of insignificance in God's scheme. It was an impression he had never before gotten, certainly not this deeply, he thought. He picked up a handful of sand, letting it fall through the end of his fist. A few grains stuck to his palm. He examined them and felt smaller than the tiniest— and *was,* he freely acknowledged, in the totality of existing things strewn throughout the universe.

It was not a feeling calculated to encourage self-confidence. Wholly intolerant of ego, denying it any right to exist. How important is any man? he mused, his eyes fixed on the North Star. Even Jesus, Mohammed, Buddha. For what are the greatest of all but what other men make of them?

He swept the sky with his hand. "It's all so huge it makes a man feel trivial as hell. Doesn't it you? It does me."

"It sometimes makes me feel like nobody or nothing even knows I'm alive. And if I stopped living nobody'd know, nothing would change, not a speck."

"I'd know, my friend."

"You'd be the only one . . . friend."

He grinned. Doc got the feeling he was a little bit embarrassed. He went on.

"When I was a little tad, still going to school, we had this teacher, Mrs. Gillespie. She was real pretty, with long black hair that kinda curled at the end and big dark eyes and the sweetest smile."

"Were you in love with her?"

"Hell no! That's not sayin' I didn't like her. Man, she was some fine teacher. She treated us more like friends she was talking to than little kids."

"She didn't talk down to you."

"Never once. Anyways, we had this globe o' the world, sitting up on the corner of her desk. You could spin it and everything and it leaned over at an angle, like the world's supposed to. One day she up and asked us, right outta the blue, 'What holds the world up in the sky?' "

"What did you say?"

"Nothin'. I never said anything in school unless I got asked straight out. Ossip Hale, he was the class big-mouth, Mr. Know-it-all. She asks and up shoots his hand. He says God is holding up the world. He's sitting in a chair, maybe even a rocker, and holding it in his lap so it won't fall down and down and down and land in hell.''

"What did Mrs. Gillespie say to that?"

"She said . . . oh man, I remember like it was yesterday because o' what she did after. She told Ossip that he could be right, that that could be one theory.''

"Didn't she say anything about the law of gravity?"

"Oh sure, that's what she was workin' up to. But you gotta understand, she was smart when it come to people's feelings. She'd never outright say 'That's wrong' or 'I don't think that's possible' or like that. She'd smile and nod like everything was possible. She asked other kids, and they had all sorts o' ideas, until one o' the girls—the girls were the real smart ones, not Ossip. He just made out like he was. One o' the girls mentions gravity. Which is how Sarah got around to explainin' it.''

"Sarah?"

"I mean Mrs. Gillespie. She got out a pin and called us all up front and we stood around the globe and she found the U.S., and Arkansas, and stuck the pin in right where Fulton County is. Where she said she figured it was, on account you couldn't see the counties. The whole state was only a little bigger than the head o' the pin. So she says 'There's Fulton County under the point, and if you use your imaginations and imagine the point spread out, you can fit Viola under it.'

"And I was standin' there and I thought what everybody else musta been thinkin', that if you spread it out even more there'd be home. There'd be our farm. What I'm gettin' at is *that* was the very first time I felt like you're talkin' about. Lotsa times since, when I'm out in the wide open spaces, especially alone.''

"You liked Sarah, didn't you?"

"I told you, she was some fine teacher. Everybody liked

her. The only time I ever saw her get really mad was when I left school for good.''

"You quit?''

"Hell, no. Ten-year-olds don't quit school. Maybe twelve, maybe thirteen. No, my father took me out the day after my tenth birthday.''

"That's right, I remember your telling me.''

"He needed me to help with the farm. Not just chores after school—full time. Even Sundays, except mornings, when we had go-to-meetin'.''

"Your father was the salt of the earth, wasn't he?''

Raider nodded. "He wrote the book on ornery. In all my years home, I can't recollect ever seeing him smile.''

"Why did your mother ever marry somebody like that?''

"Don't ask me, I wasn't around. Maybe he was different back then. Maybe kind and good to her. He was good to her when I was growing up. It was me he couldn't stomach. I never could figure it out. I never did nothing to him. Did everything he asked me. Tried like hell. The harder I tried, the more he'd, you know, demand.''

"Didn't your mother side with you?''

"Tried to. They'd argue over me something fierce. He'd always tell her he was tryin' to build my backbone.'' He grinned. "Felt more like he was tryin' to bust it. She'd argue I was just a little boy still. You know how mothers are.

"Lucky for me I was busy from sunup to sundown, outside and away from him most o' the time. We had sixty-two acres and cows to put out and bring in, hogs to slop, chickens. Mister, I sure knew what a good day's work was early on in life.

"When he got real mad at me he used to beat on me like a damn drum. I musta run away fifty times, a hundred. But I always come back, on accounta her. Then she took sick with the pneumonia and died.

"When the funeral was over, when the preacher closed the book, I took one last look at him and walked away whistlin'. He come chasin' after me. He knew what I was about. Everybody there was lookin' at us like we were loco. I mean to say, this was at a funeral. You're supposed to act, you know . . . Anyway, I got away.''

"You were thirteen.''

"And about a half. I got outta Arkansas up to Missouri. Never looked back, never went. Except once, years and years after. I went back to see my mother's and his graves. Once I was out, life got a lot better overnight, I can tell you. I made out okay on the river. Like I say, I was goin' on fourteen and tall for my age, but skinny as a rag. All bones and hair. But I was strong. I could lift and stack with the best of 'em.''

"It's a crime your having to leave school. I'll bet your mother was furious.''

"She put up a fuss, but she'd always end up givin' in. He was her husband, what else could she do? He worked the farm okay. He sure wasn't lazy, even if he was a cotton-pickin' bastard. Sunday time off for church got to be really sweet to look forward to.''

"I've heard that practically everybody in Arkansas is Baptist.''

Raider frowned. "Now you mention it, I don't even know what we were. It was just Sunday-go-to-meetin', with Bibles and hymn singin' and the preacher: Reverend Palfry. He used to scare the britches off everybody, and they loved it. He was tall and wide with big eyes and wild hair. He'd comb it, but it wouldn't stay down. When he got to shoutin' and throwin' his head around it'd fly out like a dried dandelion. He was real pale, but by the time he got done poundin' and bellowin' and throwin' his head around he'd be red all over. Anybody sit and listen to him the first time, his heart'd pound and he'd bust out in a sweat, the fear o' God was so strong, the way he shoved it into you.

"He maybe wasn't the best sin buster I ever saw, but he sure was the loudest. Shake the rafters and blow out the windows. He run off with Mrs. Sibley; she used to stand up alone and sing.''

"She was the choir.''

"Right. She had a real pretty voice. Did a great 'Bringin' In the Sheaves.' And she was good-lookin'. She and Reverend Palfry run off together. We had to get somebody to take his place. We got this old, old man. He couldn't run. Man, he could hardly walk. What about you? You've never told me nothin'—''

"About my childhood?"

"I bet you went to school till you were thirty."

"Not quite."

"I bet they don't have little red schoolhouses in Boston. Beats me where they get that little red schoolhouse thing anyway. I never saw a red one around Viola. Ours was just bare pine, inside and out; not a lick o' any color paint." His eyes softened, taking on a dreamy look. "But it was nice."

"Sarah made it nice, right?"

"Sarah Gillespie. Tell me about your schoolin'."

"It wasn't nearly as colorful as yours. I went to private school from six right up to college."

"Then what'd you do?"

"Graduated. I'd majored in English. I wanted to be a newspaperman, I thought, but it turned out I didn't have the patience, much less the ability. It may sound like sour grapes, but I've often thought since that the trouble with being a newspaperman is that you don't *make* the action, you just report it. You get there after it's happened and scribble it down and it goes into the paper and somebody reads it and throws it away. I tried different things—banking, even teaching. Office work in one sort of business or another. Business is a boring business, Rade."

"You had to have action so you joined the Pinks. Asshole."

"What about you?"

"I got no education. This is a good job for somebody with no education. But you oughta be 'shamed o' yourself."

Doc grinned. "So I'm a masochist."

"I don't know *what* I am. Baptist, I guess."

Eleventh day.

"Damn!"

So rarely did Doc swear, his outburst, mild as it was,

caused Raider to start and blink. He was sitting, inspecting his boots. The left one needed stitching up the outside near the top. He turned and saw his partner shaking his watch, holding it to his ear, muttering, shaking it a second time.

"It's stopped. Something's broken, I can hear it."

Raider grinned. "In the watch?"

"Jackass. It's not funny. I've had this watch thirteen years and it's never lost a minute."

"Doc, it's just a damn watch, it's not your son."

"You don't understand. You don't carry a watch. When you do you become dependent upon it. You rely on it. Not to know the time of day or night, especially out here at the end of the world, is annoying, frustrating."

"There's plenty other ways o' tellin' time. You look at the sun."

"I know, I know. When it's out."

"It's been out every day. Practically every hour, except that little sprinkle crossing the Basin. I wish to hell it'd go in, at least till we get outta this sand and back up into the hills."

Doc looked up at the stars. "A pity you can't tell time by the stars."

"You can."

"Rade . . ."

"I mean it. Look, see the North Star? And see the Big Dipper? It travels round it just like the hands on a clock, only backwards. Now, the handle's up and the bowl's at nine o'clock, right? That makes it just about ten P.M."

"You're pulling my leg."

"I'm not, honest. How come you don't know a simple thing like that? Every illiterate cowpuncher knows it. How do you think a man riding night herd knows when to come off shift? The Big Dipper goes round the North Star one full circle every twenty-four hours. You watch: When it's moved down to about eight, it'll be midnight."

"I'll have to miss it. I'll be asleep."

"So what do you care what time it is? Listen to me, it'll keep coming down. If you should wake up and see it sittin' like a pan on a stove with the North Star above it a little off to the right, it'll be four in the mornin'. You check, you'll see if you're awake.''

"That's all very fascinating, but I'd still like to find somebody who can repair my watch when we get to Rosales. Is that possible?''

"Sure. Only we got other things to do when we get down there.''

"Will we ever?'' Doc sighed, shook his head, paused, listened as he shook his watch one last time, then thrust it into his shirt pocket.

"Three days. Four at the most,'' said Raider.

"You sound very sure. How do you know we're even heading in the right direction? Have you ever been there?''

"I been over to Chihuahua, and the signs are all right, the landmarks.'' He knelt beside Doc, smoothed out the sand, and drew a line. "This is the Rio Conchos, okay? Now, you know we already passed the Cerro del Barrison. It's by far the highest mountain all the way down. Now we're past it, we're keeping it off our right shoulders behind us. Chihuahua's almost straight south on a line with it and El Paso, but Rosales is off to our right. So we'll pass by Chihuahua without getting anywhere near, but we'll start seein' road arrows pointin' west tomorrow. You watch. The Rio Conchos is our best landmark. We come to more hills.''

"Mountains, Rade.''

"Not real high.''

"I'll be glad to get out of this desert. We're almost out of water. Those two aren't camels.''

"They can travel thirsty. For a while. We'll find water in the hills. And on the other side we'll cross the Rio Conchos. We're in good shape, Doc, we are. We should make Rosales in fourteen days, fifteen at the most. That beats three weeks, right?''

"Tomorrow's the twelfth.''

"We can't do anything about that, just keep goin'.''

Doc got to his feet, dusting off his denims, looking about. "This Rosales. To your knowledge is it the biggest town down there?''

"Nope. There's a much bigger one 'cross the river."

Doc brightened. "The Rio Conchos?"

"The San Pedro Delicias. It's below it."

"You're saying Rosales is on one side and the other town's on the other? That's good. Excellent!"

"We don't have to cross the river. Rosales is on this side."

Doc had crouched by Raider's drawing in the sand. "That's not what I'm getting at. You said Thatcher told you old man Clancy was down near Rosales. As things turned out it was the only thing worthwhile you got out of him." He drew a line and made an X on one side, then the other. "Here's the bigger town. The river runs between. That cuts our search area in half. Thatcher only said Rosales. That's got to mean *this side of the San Pedro*."

"Right. That's a break. We could find Clancy and old A.P. the same day we get there. If we're lucky."

They got out their bedrolls and retired for the night. The last thing Doc saw before dropping off was the Big Dipper–North Star clock. He studied their relative positions for fully a minute before deciding that it was very close to ten o'clock.

"Rade, what time would you say it is?"

Raider responded with a loud snuffling sound, then resumed snoring.

Doc woke just before dawn. The sky was lightening, graying over the mountains far away to the east. But the sky was not the first thing he recognized as his eyes slowly opened. It merely provided background for the scorpion.

Doc was lying on his left side, facing the dead fire, his clothes rolled into a ball and set in a hollow in the sand for a pillow. An inch from the tip of his nose, less, he instantly estimated, squatted the scorpion, its tail upraised, waving slowly, poised to attack.

Doc froze.

Its claws curled around, coming together, pincers almost meeting, almost touching him. They were a reddish-brown, bristled, and sharply horned where they joined its body. Two yellow eyes set close together in a patch darker-colored than the surrounding shell fixed on him.

One antenna brushed his cheek, then the other.

He clenched his teeth, his heart pounding in his chest. His forehead, his face felt hot, then cool, clammy, as sweat burst from his pores. Again an antenna brushed his cheek lightly. At the same time its tail rose, coming closer, threatening, threatening. . . .

"Rade."

Raider snored on.

"Rade."

No response. Doc could not see his partner, lying less than ten feet away on the other side of the ashes. He could only focus on the scorpion. The continuing rhythmic movement of its appendages mesmerized him.

For a long moment eyes locked; they stared at one another. Doc began drawing in air, filling his lungs. Jerked his head back. Rolled over. Scrambled to his feet. He'd snapped his neck. It felt like it. Hurt like hell. He kicked his bedroll over the thing. He began stomping on it. Fiercely. Violently. Like a man suddenly crazed. Cursing.

Raider woke, sitting up.

"What the . . ."

"Scorpion!"

To his surprise Doc could scarcely speak, fear constricting his throat, his voice captured by a series of gasps. He stopped stomping and stood shaking, swallowing hard, rubbing the back of his neck with one hand, pointing at his would-be attacker under the blanket and soogan with the other.

"Jesus," muttered Raider.

He got up, stretched, came over and jerked the covers back. The scorpion lay on its back, crushed and broken in two. He stared down at it. A smile started, spreading over his face.

"For Chrissakes, Doc!"

"It . . . it was practically perched on my nose ready to strike. Good God, it came that close!"

"Strike, my ass. I hate to tell you, but that's no scorpion."

"Raider, I know a scorpion when I see one."

"It's a damn vinegarroon. It can spray and stink, but it can't hurt you any more than a housefly, for Chrissakes."

"It's no vinegarroon, it's a scorpion."

"Whip scorpion. It's harmless. Look at the tail. It's long and skinny like a whip. Not thick like a scorpion's. There's no bulb at the tip, nothin' to hold poison. No stinger. Couldn't you see?"

"It woke me up. It was the first thing I saw. It scared the living daylights out of me."

"Poor little fella, you just had to kill him, didn't you."

"Oh, shut up!"

"Don't you want to know why they call it a vinegarroon?"

"Not especially, but I'm sure you'll tell me."

"It squirts vinegar."

"Nonsense."

"Stuff that smells like it. Can't hurt you."

"I know. You keep saying that. I didn't recognize my first vinegarroon. Can you forgive me? Can you find it in your heart? Let's pack up and get out of here." Doc winced as he massaged his neck.

"Aren't you hungry after all that exercise? Don't you want breakfast? Nice hot coffee?"

"You expect me to eat after this? Are you insane? I have absolutely no appetite for anything, least of all that aciduous sludge you call coffee. You eat. I'll tend to the horses."

Thirteenth day.

The sun hung directly overhead, its position serving to remind Doc of the condition of his watch. They were in the mountains; men and horses were weary, their slow progress southward down the central highlands bringing them closer and closer to exhaustion.

They had stopped by a mountain stream. The water crashing over the rugged limestone bed fringed and dotted with club moss was ice cold. The horses drank greedily. Raider pulled back the mare.

"Easy, little girl, you'll get cramps."

Kneeling, drenching his face beside the drinking pinto, Doc paused and lifted the horse's head. The sun sent down golden shafts, binding the luxuriant growth to the heavens. A flock of early arriving grebes, their necks long and slender, their black and white plumage blending in shadow against the sun, hurtled by overhead.

The Pinkertons rested and ate. Doc had come to detest the taste of beans, the faintest smell of them—hot, lukewarm, cold, congealed in the sludge of their own juices; loathed and despised them. When they got to Rosales he would eat tamales, the hotter the better. Tacos, enchiladas, anything, everything edible. But not beans.

Three hours later found them descending a slope toward another stream situated less than a quarter mile from level ground. It flowed laterally, almost horizontally, idling along, belting the mountain. They followed its course until it began to lower gradually, seeking the plain below. Unlike the stream higher up, its banks were barren of trees and companion undergrowth, with only moss and a few broken reeds to be seen.

Again they stopped to drink. The water was shallow, sparkling in the sunlight. Behind them, imbedded in the slope, a ledge fully twenty feet long jutted forward, its base deeply eroded eons earlier by the stream, which had carved an overhang. On the opposite side of the river the barren surface was strewn with boulders. Beyond them the pines and shrubs reclaimed the mountain. Raider and Doc knelt beside the stream on a flat rock that dipped into it, bottomed it, and reappeared on the opposite bank like a shallow basin shoved into the water.

A shot blasted, echoing among the rocks, the slug striking midway between the two men, positioned less than two feet apart. The horses, who were also drinking, jerked up their heads, the whites of their eyes showing. Doc and Raider had thrown themselves backwards, scrambling on all fours, pulling their mounts so hard they nearly stripped the bits from their mouths, hauling them under the overhang as bullets rained down.

Silence. Broken only by the gentle movement of the stream. The horses stood stiffly, expectantly, their eyes still fearful.

"Hey, Yanqui, welcome to Mehico!"

So high-pitched was the voice, for a moment Raider imagined a woman was calling down. Raucous laughter followed.

"Hey, Yanqui, we wan' your horses, your guns an' your dollars. You give us them an' we let you go. What you say?"

Still gripping the mare's reins, Raider backed slowly out from under the ledge and lifted his head so that he could be heard, the top of his hat poking up, showing.

"Your mother's a whore!"

A second furious volley as he ducked.

"Yanqui bastard! For the las' time, we wan' your horses, your guns an' your dollars. You wan' to live or to die? What you say?"

Again, up came the crown of Raider's hat.

"Your father's a pimp!"

A third fusillade, battering the ledge above their heads.

"Rade," said Doc in exasperation, "there are times when I honestly think you're certifiably insane. What in God's name are you trying to do, get our heads blown off?"

Raider had taken off his hat. A shot had pierced the top of the crown. Poking a finger through it, he waggled it.

"How they going to hit us through two feet o' ledge? Answer me that."

"They've got us pinned down like butterflies on a board. They can wait us out till doomsday."

"That's why I'm doin' what I'm doin', goddamn it! Whoever's up there has to be assholes to throw down lead like it was rocks. Which is exactly what I'm tryin' to make 'em do, if it's okay with you."

"And get yourself killed in the process."

Again he waggled his finger. "This? It's nothin', just a little fresh-air ventilation."

"Yanquiiiiiiiii . . ."

"You throttle your lizard!" roared Raider.

A long silence.

"What you say?"

"You jerk, you play . . ." Raider paused. "Get out that lingo book. Look up Spanish for jerkin' off."

"Don't be ridiculous. Besides, the book is only phrases, conversational, it's not a dictionar—"

Down came another volley.

"How many do you think there are?" Doc asked.

Raider responded with a disdainful scowl. "How the hell am I supposed to know? Could be five, ten."

"Could be only a couple, firing with both hands."

"Don't bet on that."

"Well, I suppose we have to play. Let's get out the Winchesters."

"For sure. You sure can't hope to hit anythin' at this range with that dumb .38 Diamondback." He laughed. "I bet it can't even reach that high." He sobered. "It's times like this you make me goddamn mad. When the hell are you gonna break down and buy yourself a man-size gun?"

Doc ignored him. He had set about getting his rifle out of his bedroll.

"We'll get 'em out, keep 'em handy. But don't you go usin' yours."

"Why, pray tell, not?"

"They seen our gear packed behind our cantles, but they couldn't see the rifles, all wrapped up the way we got 'em. Why don't we let 'em think all we got is six-guns? With all their firepower they could get careless."

Doc considered this. He nodded. Raider looked to his right.

"You stick here. I'm going over behind that rock and give 'em a little o' what they're askin' for. Hang onto my rifle. If I want it, toss it over."

"Hadn't you better stay put?"

"Doc, this rock is like a damn roof. There's no way we can shoot back without backin' off and showin' ourselves. We do, and they'll cut us down like cornstalks."

"We can work out of the ends."

"Do it."

Abandoning the overhang, Raider flung himself behind the boulder located just beyond the end of the overhang. Slugs came down, singing off the rock as he briefly showed himself. Scrunching down, he edged around the boulder. Sunlight struck a gun barrel high above, vanishing as quickly as it appeared. He threw three quick shots at the spot and pulled back. A cry of pain came drifting down on the breeze. He snaked around the other side for a look. A man lay draped over a boulder, his sombrero fallen off and tumbling down, bouncing lightly off one rock, then another, his lifeless hands hanging limply, his pistol dropping to the rocks below. Satisfaction mingling with pride warmed Raider. He strained his ears. He could faintly hear cursing, arguing, and what sounded like sobbing.

"Somebody up there's crying," remarked Doc.

Raider grinned. "Must be a close relative o' the recently deceased."

"Hey, Yanqui, you dead, you dead!"

And down came another loud waste of ammunition. Doc had hobbled both horses and scuttled under the ledge to the opposite end. He sneaked a quick peek. Six shots greeted his appearance. Raider returned the honors, drawing more fire. He guessed there were four of them, five at most. Not particularly inviting odds, but the lucky location of the ledge helped to offset them. He glanced over at the horses. They pawed the ground nervously, their eyes still huge, filled with fear. They were safe enough, he thought. Even out in the open they wouldn't be hit. They were too valuable. The bunch up top wanted them, and healthy. As much as they wanted him and Doc dead.

Doc was firing and got return fire. He recoiled, pulling back, his right hand going to his jaw. Slowly he brought it down. He was bleeding; a bullet had grazed the base of his cheek. Another inch and it would have broken his jaw and lodged in his lower throat. A bloody line the size of his little finger showed.

"For Chrissakes be more careful!" snarled Raider.

"Yanquis! You are outnumber ten to one. You throw out your guns an' show yourself with your hands high up an' we call it off. No more shootin'! Nobody get hurt! You walk away."

"I don't believe this asshole," said Raider. "He's settin' himself up for us. Talk about playin' ball . . ."

"Don't count your chickens, Rade."

Up on his feet, Raider ducked and ran back to the cover of the ledge. Doc joined him.

It's a deal!" called Raider. *"No more shootin'!"*

"No more!"

"Promise?"

"I swear by the Holy Virgin!"

"He has to be a good soul at heart, Rade."

"You bet. Let's do it."

They tossed out their six-guns, which clattered to rest on top of the ledge.

"Very good, amigos! Now, back out where we can see you."

They had been side by side when they tossed out their guns. Readying their rifles, they moved to opposite ends of the ledge. Doc pulled his blood-smeared hand down from his face.

"You okay?" asked Raider.

"Rade, what are we doing here? How come these things always, but always, happen to us?"

"Just luck."

"Show yourself, amigos! Look, see, we lay down our guns!"

Raider squinched his eyes and grinned. "I'll count three," he said. "We'll pour it to 'em. You work your side, I'll keep my fire right o' center. Here we go. One, two . . ."

Another fusillade rang down.

"Show yourself, or we come down an' kill you!"

"No, no!" bellowed Raider. *"You promised!"* He glanced at Doc. "One, two, three."

Each raked his side, thirty-four rounds slamming into the site. Two of the attackers had obligingly revealed themselves.

Both were hit immediately. The survivors fled. So quickly, there was no telling how many there were.

"Get the guns," said Doc tiredly. "I'll ready the horses."

"You oughta wash that out, Doc. Put some cobwebs on it, stop the bleedin'."

"Do you see any barns around here?"

"Just tryin' to be helpful."

"I know, I know. I'm sorry, Rade, I guess I'm just overly frazzled by all this. This"—he jerked his head upward chin first—"is the last straw."

"Take it easy. We don't need cobwebs. We can burn some wood and rub on the ashes. That always works. Hey, Doc."

"What is it?"

"We're gettin' close, you know? Just past those trees and down to the plain we should be able to see the Conchos. We just follow it on down. Less than fifty miles and we'll be in Rosales."

CHAPTER FIFTEEN

Fourteenth day.

They saw their fourth rude, lopsided arrow sign indicating the city of Chihuahua as they followed the Conchos down. Late in the afternoon, at Raider's suggestion, they stopped to take a swim. The water was muddy but refreshing, not nearly as cold as the mountain streams. Cold enough, until both got used to it. Doc's wound had clotted. Ducking again and again, he rinsed off what remained of the ashes Raider had applied.

Continuing on, they crossed the western branch of the river at a shallow spot, roughly midway between Aldama and Chihuahua. Late in the afternoon they met an old Indian, sitting under an outrageously battered straw hat, perched on his burro with pairs of jugs yoked in front and back of him. He was slightly drunk, but his eyes were bright in his face. He was barefoot, and his well-worn clothes hung on his skinny frame like a rag on a stick. He hailed them and they pulled up.

"*Chona*," he said, obviously pleased to meet somebody. "*Chona, Chona!*"

"Hello, hello," said Doc pleasantly.

Raider greeted the man.

" 'Allo," said the man and grinned. There wasn't a tooth in his mouth.

Doc got out his phrase book.

"That's not gonna do you any good," said Raider. "I bet he doesn't know two words o' Spanish. He's an Indian, maybe Tarahumara."

The old man had pulled the stopper on one of his reed-wrapped jugs. He raised it and drank, the liquor trickling down from the corners of his mouth. He offered the jug to Raider, who was closest to him. Raider took it.

"Good old tarantula juice. *Aguardiente,* most likely. Three swigs and you'll either fall off your horse or fly into Rosales." He smelled the liquor and grimaced. "Pulque." He offered the jug to Doc. "Have a snort. Tastes like sour milk, but it's good for you."

"I'll pass. You ought to, you and your touchy stomach."

Raider shook his head, swigged, pinched his eyes shut, swallowed hard, winced, and opened his eyes.

"Not bad."

He took another swig, repeating the pantomime of suffering, than handed the jug back, thanking the man profusely. Doc pointed ahead.

"Rosales?"

"Meoqui." The old man nodded vigorously.

"What's Meoqui?" Doc asked Raider. "Could it be yes?"

"I think it's another town."

"Meoqui," repeated the man, turning, pointing down the road. He then shifted his hand a little to the left. "Rosales."

"Excellent," said Doc. "How far?"

The man stared at him blankly. Raider dismounted and drew a line on the ground with the fold of his reins. He marked a point close to his foot.

"Us here. Here." He pointed at the mark and at them. "Rosales here. Rosales. Rosales." He made a mark at the other end of the line. He shifted his finger between one and the other, back and forth. "Here, Rosales, here, Rosales." He gestured the line connecting the two.

The old man nodded. He pointed to the sun, which was sinking into the Sierra Madres. He mimed darkness setting in.

They thanked him, waved good-bye and went on. The sun slipped lower, sending vivid purple streaks out left and right, capping the mountains like colored snow. The river passed them silently on its way north, and the visitant darkness arrived and conquered the land.

• • •

They reached Rosales near ten o'clock, by Doc's reckoning, reading the Big Dipper–North Star clock. It was small—much smaller than he had pictured it. It came up to them abruptly, rising like a cluster of mushrooms out of the earth. Dotting the darkness were myriad lanterns. The tallest building was the church; no surprise to Doc, although he had never before set foot in Mexico, and had read and knew little about the country. The steeple stood against the stars, the town assembled before it.

The street down which they rode was more a wide gutter, strewn with rocks, rendered slightly concave by traffic and flanked by poinsettia and mango trees; organ cactus planted side by side, forming fences; and tall, unidentifiable shrubs. Through the growing walls they could see tile-roofed little huts constructed of black adobe bricks. Lanterns and candles glowed within. A dog came running out, skidded to a stop, and barked loudly at the horses, causing the mare to shy.

They came into the plaza. It was tiny, compared to the center of Santa Fe, with a lonely fountain standing in the center, the water burbling softly into the stone basin ringing it. All around the plaza was gaily lit, a dozen cantinas and restaurants hosting patrons; music, laughter, and babble. Wedged between them, the shops and other business establishments were shuttered for the night.

The men wore white cotton clothes, some with their big hats on, others clutching them or hanging them on a knob on the back of their chair on the sidewalk in front of the cantinas. Nobody they could see was without a hat, no man. The women in their tight white tops and long skirts wore flowers—in their hair, hiding their ears, around their necks, borrowing from nature to look their prettiest: bougainvillea, hibiscus, roses. The air was warm, heavy, with a floral scent, the breeze coming off the river behind the church capturing the fragrances of the flowers, carrying and blending them.

They found a stable and gave over the horses, buying fresh oats for them. Both gobbled them voraciously.

"Two weeks o' grass and these two'll eat up the bucket," observed Raider.

"They've lost weight," said Doc.

"So have we."

Doc made a face. The odor in the stable was so overpowering it set his eyes to watering. The man in charge sat outside on a broken-backed chair, dozing. He had their money and was ostensibly too tired for conversation beyond pleasantries and the brief discussion of the needs of their horses, to which conversation both Pinkertons contributed from their respective meager stores of Spanish.

They crossed the narrow street and stood in the shadows.

"I want two things only," said Doc, "a hot meal and a bed. A real bed: feather mattress, a soft pillow. Two pillows."

"How about a canopy and a bell cord for the maid and breakfast in the mornin'? You find a feather bed in this town and I'll eat it. Speakin' of which, I'm starving. Let's eat, something besides Mex strawberries."

"Strawberries?"

"Beans, Doc, beans."

They started back toward the plaza, the sounds of music and laughter assuring the right direction.

"Rade, we've got to get hold of a local, somebody who can speak English, somebody we can trust."

"That rules out the police."

"No policeman, even an honest one. We ring them in and we'll get all tangled up."

"Old man Clancy could have this whole town in his back pocket, you know that? Bought and paid for."

"I doubt it. Why should he bother? I'll bet he's holed up somewhere nearby and just sends into town for anything he needs. He's probably never even shown his face here."

"Everything he needs, includin' a firin' squad for A.P."

"Not funny. I think I know how to approach this thing, getting help. Whoever it is, we'll have to pay him, of course."

"Doc, money isn't gonna buy honesty. It never does."

"Leave it to me."

They stopped by the first cantina they came to, but it was

crowded, with every table occupied. They moved on. The second cantina was smaller, but half the tables were empty. They stood outside looking in. A boy was sitting just inside the door, flailing away at a guitar.

"You suppose the food's any good?" asked Raider. "I told you I can't stand hot stuff. Some o' their chili peppers are guaranteed to blow holes in your gut."

"We'll be careful what we order. Come on."

"Señores."

A man came up to them, doffing his hat, smiling, revealing missing teeth. His nose was huge. It looked as if it had been hastily molded out of putty and slapped into place. It spread with his smile, nearly doubling in width. His nostrils were enormous, resembling the muzzles of a double-barreled shotgun. His belly showed from under the end of his shirt. His huaraches were so old they were coming apart, and with every step they creaked loudly. The sound resembled that of a chair being rocked on a hardwood floor.

"Americanos, eh? Just arrived, eh? Welcome to Rosales. I am Miguel. Miguel Angel Donoso, but everybody calls me Galo. Miguel, Galo. Understand? You going into this place? You don't want to go in here, the cockroaches are big as your thumbs. The wife of the owner cooks them into the tacos de pollo, tamales, everything. You come with me and I introduce you to the best food in Rosales, the best in all of Chihuahua. Just down to the corner, Amilamia's. My wife. It is her restaurant; she owns it. I help run it. The food is magnificent, fit for Presidente Díaz himself. You come with me, all right? I am Miguel Angel Donoso, but everybody calls me Galo. Right this way."

Getting a word in appeared impossible. The man talked nonstop, and his smile remained stuck to his face. He did not wheedle, he did not cajole, he overflowed with good fellowship. He had worked in Texas for three years, he told them, in Presidio, across the Rio Grande from Ojinaga.

"Right where the Conchos flows into the Bravo. Of course you call it Rio Grande. So I will call it Rio Grande to be hospitable. Right this way, right here. Here we are."

He herded them inside the little restaurant. It was half-filled with patrons. There was no music. A stern-looking woman with magnificent hair falling down her back to below her waist stood behind the bar. She glared at Galo, and smiled and nodded at Doc and Raider.

"My wife, Amilamia. She is the owner of this most marvelous restaurant. Is it not beautiful? I am the fortunate man to be the husband of the owner of this beautiful restaurant. Here, sit, sit."

He pulled back chairs, snatched up the bar rag and wiped the oilcloth.

They had *pozola* and beef cut into cubes and cooked in a surprisingly mild sauce. They had coffee with boiled milk. They also shared a bottle of mescal. Galo sat with them while they ate and his wife worked.

"What brings you gentlemen to Rosales, may I ask? I shouldn't ask, I know, it is not my business. One should never ask others what they are doing or why. I do not mean to be rude, I merely . . ."

"We're down from Texas," interrupted Doc. "From Austin."

"Ahhh, Austin, I have been to Austin. I worked for three years as a carpenter's helper in Presidio."

"You already told us," said Raider, picking his teeth with the corner of his napkin and frowning

"Yes, I did, I recall. Did I tell you . . ."

"We're with the state government," continued Doc, holding up both hands, stopping him in mid-sentence. "Governor Roberts has authorized us to come down here to locate Texans, former Texans, men who fled the country after the war to seek refuge in Mexico. We're empowered to offer them full amnesty and money to pay for their transportation home."

"But the war was a long time ago."

"A long time. Unfortunately, many of these men left wives and children. Our job is to find them and make them the offer. If they want to go back they can. If they don't . . ." He shrugged. "It's up to them. Do you know of any Americans here in Rosales?"

"No. Perhaps in Delicias, across the river. Or Meoqui, up the line."

"We already been there," said Raider. "We found two guys. Both of 'em decided to go back. We give 'em their money."

Doc nodded.

"How interesting. Yours must be fascinating work. You travel all over the country?"

"All over," said Doc. "For the last five years."

"Going on six," said Raider.

"My my my. You are dedicated men. I wish I knew some Americans. You are the first to come to Rosales in months. Wait, now I think of it, I have seen one or two gring . . . er, Americans. Two, yes, but both much too young to have fought in the war. They were in their twenties."

"Do they live in town?" Doc asked, setting the empty bottle aside and leaning across the table, suddenly interested.

"I don't think so."

"We'd like to meet them."

"But they are too young."

"But they may know somebody older, somebody who might have served in the Confederate army, somebody living not far from here."

"That is possible."

"When is the last time you saw these two?"

"A few days ago, maybe a week. I will look out for them."

"You do that. Any American you can find for us, regardless of how old he is, we'll pay you three dollars. If you find any ex-soldiers, we'll give you twenty dollars."

"Twenty!" The bloodhound eyes lit up like twin beacons.

Doc offered his hand. "Deal?"

Galo shook it so hard, Doc had to grab his wrist to restrain him.

"Sí, sí, sí, sí." He started up from his chair.

"Wait," said Doc. "One thing. All you have to do is tell us who they are and where we can find them. We'll follow up. Don't you talk to them. Don't approach them."

"The reason for that," said Raider, "is on account there may be some who when they hear about the money may pretend to be Americans. They could be from Canada or some island in the Caribbean, *entiendo*?"

"*Sí*, I understand. Trust me. When I am given a job to do, I do it right. Perfectly!"

"Galo," said Doc, "we have to contact our superiors in Austin. Inform them we've arrived here. Where's the telegraph office?"

"Across the plaza." He indicated. "But it is closed. Besides, you can't send a telegram. Not for a while. The wires between here and Chihuahua are down. There was a bad storm last week. See the roofs over there? You can see the damage. It knocked down some poles. They are still making the repairs."

Doc and Raider exchanged glances; each could see the relief in the other's eyes. The state capital was about fifty miles away. Any intelligence of what was going on at the Nebraska State Penitentiary in Lincoln and in Governor Garber's mind regarding Will Francis Clancy's sons would have to come from Chihuahua.

Galo beamed, shifting his glance between them. "It will be at least another week, they say. How about another bottle of mescal?"

"Another time," said Raider. He stretched and spoke through a yawn. "We got to get some sleep."

"Do you have an extra room?" asked Doc. "We'll pay, of course."

Galo shook his head. "My sister Micaela and her little boy from Durango are staying with us. But Esperanza Julia Veñas across the way . . . See that house with the wide door? It is red. You can't see it in the shadows, but it is. She has rooms to let. Very comfortable, clean. We always recommend Señora Veñas's rooms for visitors. She is a good friend of my wife's, a widow. Her husband was shot by the police. He was a bad one. She has fourteen rooms. A very large house, very profitable. She and her sister Rosita run the place. Things are quiet in town. Next week is our fiesta in honor of Our Lady of the Rosary. The farmers and their families flock in from all over; the town is bursting with humanity; the plaza is so crowded you can't get a burro from one end to the other. But that is next week, starting Tuesday. The rooms are small, but very clean. Immaculate. You will . . .''

Again Doc held up both hands, stemming the verbal torrent. Galo stopped his tongue. "Let's go see the señora, okay?" All three rose from their chairs, Doc counting out money, laying it on the table. "One last question."

"Ask me anything, I know everything."

"Is there a watchmaker in town?"

"You want a watch made?"

"Fixed."

Galo's eyebrows came together, his mouth drooped, he shook his head. "In Delicias across the river, perhaps. Not Rosales." He shrugged and grinned. "Few of us have watches or clocks. There is a clock in Ignacio Lopez Gallardo's shop window down the street. He sells silver and jewelry, all kinds of religious articles. Ah, but perhaps I can help. I am very mechanical. I was a carpenter's helper in Presidio for three years. I have a certain flair with machines."

"Thanks just the same, but it can wait."

"Yeah," said Raider. "You're gonna be too busy. Let's go. I got to lie down before I fall down."

Esperanza Julia Veñas was strikingly beautiful, even awakened out of her beauty sleep. She was bleary-eyed and very close to furious at their intrusion. The room given them was small; the ceiling rose to barely two inches above Raider's head, prompting him to duck slightly as they came in. The beds were . . .

"Only a little softer than the desert," he observed, testing his mattress. "So much for your feathers and two pillows. No vinegarroons or cockroaches, though. That's a help."

Doc stripped to the waist and washed in the wooden basin half filled with tepid water from an enormous pitcher. He studied his image in the mirror.

"I look marvelous. We should have left a call; we could

fall asleep and not wake up for three days. Hey, things look like they're turning around a little bit, don't they? What do you think?''

"You mean 'cause we got down here in one piece? We haven't even started lookin'.''

"I'm talking about finding Galo.''

"We didn't find nobody, he found us. Happens all the time here. We come walkin' into the plaza and everybody sees we're gringos. There's always somebody who can speak English comes runnin' up all smiles and welcomin' and chompin' at the bit to take your money. Twenty dollars. Man, you sure got a charitable nature. For half that he woulda been willin' to walk to Chihuahua to pick you up cheroots.''

"We can afford him.''

"But can we trust him?''

"What do you think?''

"I don't think nothin'. I just met him. Besides, it's not just whether he's on the up and up, but whether he's got brains enough for the job. He sure has a hard time stoppin' talking. And he's a real pro at stickin' his foot in his mouth.''

"My instincts tell me he's going to work out famously. He'll be a big help.''

"Your instincts are tellin' you what you want to hear, what you hope.''

Doc got into bed, listening to his partner's continuing spate of pessimism. Although he didn't take it seriously, he had no difficulty tolerating it; their long association reminded him that he should expect it. Raider had drained every drop from the small well of his optimism over the course of the past fourteen days; longer, actually: ever since Rawlins. His supply exhausted, a change had to come, a reversal. Unlike most people, he was neither consistently pessimistic or optimistic. For some unknown reason he invariably found it necessary to compensate, to turn his attitude inside out and effect a balance between the two.

On he rambled. Doc closed his eyes and opened the door in his mind to let in sleep.

"It's been four whole days since the hangings. I mean you

can't rule out Governor What's-his-name goin' ahead like he promised. Chrissakes, the odds against us pullin' this off are gettin' longer every hour passes. I figure 'em about ten to one, and by this time tomorrow, fifteen, maybe even twenty. All we got workin' for us is those telegraph lines bein' down. And maybe not that. Could be old man Clancy sent one o' his crew up to Chihuahua with orders to sit in the telegraph office and keep up contact with whoever's up in Lincoln knows what's goin' on. It makes sense he'd have somebody up there to keep him in the know.

"And as far as Commodore Vanderbilt or Chief Justice Waite stickin' their oar in to save A.P.'s hide, they could do it, sure. Likely already have, but that doesn't say that Governor What's-his-name is gonna listen. I mean if he was worried about the chief's friends he wouldn'ta set the date for the executions in the first place, would he?"

Doc mumbled.

"What'd you say?"

"I said good night, Galo."

"Galo? What are you callin' me that for? I mean we got problems piled up to our ears. We got to kick 'em around, don't we? Besides—"

"Rade, for Christ's sakes, will you shut up and go to sleep?"

"Okay, okay."

CHAPTER SIXTEEN

The sun blazed, bleaching the sky, losing itself in its own brilliance. The distant mountains were dressed in pine, cobalt blue under their peaks, lightening to cornflower blue as the eye descended, lowering to the dazzlingly bright reddish and yellow browns of the valley. Scattered about like sugar cubes were houses attached to green rectangles of farmland.

They were on the road they had followed into town the previous night. They passed a woman dressed entirely in black perched on a little gray burro, its head bobbing as it pulled itself forward. She did not look at them; they could not see her face buried in the folds of her hood. Doc stood up in his stirrups, grimacing.

"I am sore. It feels like the next bounce and I'll split."

"Tighten your belt. I feel good. Good sleep, good breakfast. New man. Get your mind off your can. Let's figure how we're gonna work this."

"We'll cut off the road up ahead there and start circling the town, I guess. How can they call a village a town?"

"Villages got fifty or sixty people; there got to be at least three hundred in Rosales. Man, it is bright out." Raider pulled the front of his hat down another two inches. "I wish we had us a pair o' binoculars. We can't get too close to places. Clancy'll spot us in a second like we are. We shoulda' got us serapes, cotton pants, and big, floppy straw hats."

"I'm sorry, peons don't ride around on sixty-dollar horses."

They reached the turnoff, reined left, and headed across the valley. They passed a roadside shrine, its interior deeply shadowed, a cross mounted on a large oblong stone. Before it

144

candles were set. Above the entrance a large crack divided the center of the arch, climbing to the top and a second, smaller cross mounted there. To their right as they passed the shrine, a quarter mile distant, they could see a farmer working his field, pushing a crude wooden plow behind his oxen. Directly ahead, the mountains rose, bringing the scattered white buildings closer.

They scouted a total of twenty-three houses, observing enough activity to assure Doc, at least, that no one other than farmers and their families occupied them. Overhead the sun gradually took on color and form, the blazing whiteness of early morning giving way to a pale blue; cirrus clouds feathered the horizon.

Midday came and went. They searched on. The sun had passed its zenith and was well started down the sky when Raider reined up. They could see the town bunched at the edge of the valley below, some four or five miles distant. Beyond it, the San Pedro curled lazily, and beyond *it,* slightly blurred to the eye, lay Delicias.

"This is bullshit, Doc. We could traipse all over the slope, one end o' the valley to the other, and never find nothin'. They could be holed up in any one o' the houses we already waited round lookin' at. Sure, we see people comin' and goin', but that doesn't prove nothin'. They could be in one room, never comin' outside. What we should be doin' is searchin' every room in every damn house."

"How can we possibly do that? With what authority?"

"The man's a prisoner, his life's at stake."

"The only way we can do that would be to ring in the law. We decided not to, remember?"

"So maybe we were wrong."

"No, Rade, we can't just blunder into a house and start searching. Clancy has to be keeping his eyes peeled. He knows somebody's going to try to rescue the chief. He'd spot us long before we saw him."

"We don't even know what the bastard looks like, that's what really makes this ridiculous."

"Frustrating."

"That too. We gotta work out something better than this. Let's head back. We'll find fatso and see if he's come up with anything."

"Maybe it's time we told him the truth, that we're looking for a man in his late sixties, early seventies, that all we know for a fact is that his face is deeply lined."

"Oh for Chrissakes! What old man's face isn't? Every damn farmer's! And that's what Clancy was before he went into the easy-money business. Deeply lined, shit!"

A mariachi band was performing in the plaza, attracting a large crowd, trumpets, guitars, and violins blending in song, the musicians in huge sombreros, frilly shirts, and tight dark suits adorned with silver. The entire town appeared to have gathered in the plaza. Those who were not standing watching the performance were shopping or standing or strolling about. The church doors stood open, and parishioners coming from confession or their daily prayers were descending the steps.

"Looks like a rehearsal for the fiesta," observed Doc.

Raider was shading his eyes from the sun and staring at the telegraph office on the far side of the fountain that had been pointed out for them by Galo the night before. It appeared to be closed.

"I wish to hell it was fiesta," he said grimly. "Everybody from the farms'd be comin' to town, all the houses'd be empty. We'd be able to turn the whole area upside down."

"There's Galo talking to his wife."

"Listenin', you mean. She looks like she's givin' him hell." Raider snickered. "I bet he hasn't done a day's sweat work since he come back from Presidio back when. These guys all live off their women if they can."

"He's working, Rade. For us."

They dismounted, tying the horses to wall rings where the street entered the plaza. Galo greeted them effusively, breaking away from his wife, running toward them. His expression suggested he was grateful for their arrival, providing as it did temporary deliverance from her nagging.

"Señors, señors! You were lucky, yes? You found—"

"We were lucky, no," interrupted Doc. He pulled him to one side. "How did you do?"

"I spread the word, all over. Others have seen the two young Americans, many people. But not the last few days. I think maybe they have left the area." He brightened. "But I have some good news. The repairs on the telegraph wires will be completed by tonight. You will be able to send your message to Chihuahua, to El Paso, and up to Austin. Is that not good?"

"Yeah," said Raider. "That's great."

"You must be hungry after riding around all morning. Come, you must eat."

They started toward Amilamia's. The band had stopped playing. The musicians were talking to the people and checking their instruments. A disturbance arose on the other side. The crowd gathered around it in seconds, so that Raider and Doc couldn't make out the cause. They ran across the plaza.

A cart had broken down; a wheel had fallen off. An old woman had been driving. She stood gesticulating angrily, the black rebozo piled on her head bobbing. Beside her in a dirty ocher-colored serape stood a man a foot and a half taller than she, despite his drooping posture. The wheel lay on the ground, the cart tilted alongside. It was carrying a load of earthen jars, three of which had broken, spilling milk down onto the wheel and puddling the ground. Galo broke through the crowd.

"Señora Moralitos," he burst above the chattering circling the scene. "Mariano, Timoteo, Señor Epopee . . ." Sputtering Spanish, he quickly took charge, drafting a half-dozen men, directing them in raising the cart, while two others reset the wheel. Another man got out a knife, cut a piece of wood from the underside edge of the cart, shaped it, and inserted it in the hole at the end of the axle tree to secure the wheel.

"That will hold it until it can be properly repaired," Galo informed them.

He took off his hat. "Permit me to introduce Mama Eufrasia Carlota Hortensia Florentina Moralitos, the sainted sister of my wife's grandmother. She sells eggs and milk. She is eighty-two years old. This is her grandson Cosme Luis. A good boy, a good worker, but not very bright. He helps her, as you can see.''

The wheel restored, the incident at an end, the crowd began breaking up. Galo clapped his hands and whistled for attention, getting it, and loudly introduced Raider and Doc.

Doc rolled his eyes and Raider tossed up his hands; but now started, there was no stopping Galo. Center stage was his, and he was determined to keep it. He carried on loudly.

''What's he saying?'' asked Doc. He had gotten out his phrase book and was turning pages back and forth confusedly.

''He's likely tellin' 'em about us, right? Askin' if anybody's seen the two young gringos. Give him that picture of A.P., why don't you? The one we got off the front page o' *Leslie's*.''

Doc unfolded the picture of Allan Pinkerton and handed it to Galo.

''We're looking for this man,'' he explained. ''Fifty dollars to whoever recognizes him and can lead us to where he is.''

''Fifty!'' Galo's eyes bulged as they lit up.

As did Raider's.

''What the hell you talkin' about, fifty bucks?''

''A hundred, Rade, five hundred, a thousand if we can find out where they've got him. Don't interrupt, don't say anything. Galo, make it a hundred.''

''Hundred? *Madre de Dios!* You're making my heart jump out of my chest. That is more money than anyone here earns in a year.''

The crowd was gaping at him expectantly. He raised both hands. He translated. They oohed and ahhed. A number of them stepped forward, waving their hands like schoolchildren, crowding around him. Including the old woman. Her grandson stood behind her. He had raised his head, as if the tumult going on around them had awakened him. For the first time Doc could see his face. It was as blank as an unminted coin, his eyes empty. Was he, he wondered, ''not very bright,'' as Galo had described him, retarded, or a qualified imbecile?

It appeared that almost everyone had seen the two young

Americans around town. No one had seen them recently. No one recognized Allan Pinkerton from his picture. Galo held it up, swinging it slowly around. Doc's glance drifted to the old woman. She was eighty-two easily, her face a mass of wrinkles. A thought had crossed her mind, brightening her black eyes. She began jabbering to Galo, grabbing his arm, squeezing it.

"What'd she say?" asked Raider. "She's seen him?"

"She's seen an old man, much older than the two—"

"*Cara de cuero, cara de cuero,*" shrilled the woman, rotating her hand in front of her face.

"What's that?" asked Raider.

Doc was leafing through his book, stopping, running his finger down the page.

"Leather face," said Galo. He shrugged. He obviously didn't understand. "He *is* an old man, whoever he is, and American."

Raider snatched the picture from him, holding it directly in front of the woman.

"*Este, este?*"

Her mouth moved, revealing itself in among her wrinkles, the corners turning down. She shook her head resolutely.

"Shit!"

Doc had closed his book. "Rade."

"What?"

"Did you hear what she said? *Cara—*"

"*Cara de cuero,*" interrupted Galo. "Leather face."

A devilish look was materializing on Doc's face. "Leather face. Where have we heard that before?"

"Thatcher," snapped Raider. "That's what he called Clancy, that night he swallowed the newspaper picture. Old leather face."

The old woman had hold of Galo's sleeve as she talked to him.

"She says she delivers milk and eggs to him every Wednesday and Saturday. To a house up in the hills. She says his face is covered with leather, a mask of leather. It is strapped to his head and only his eyes can be seen. But even without seeing his face, she can tell he is old: the way he stands, his hands . . .''

"I'll be goddamned," gasped Raider.

Doc nodded. "Old leather face. *Thatcher was speaking literally*. Telling us without even knowing it, the stupid fool.''

"Could be Clancy burned himself real bad, made himself look, you know . . .''

"Gruesome.''

"So ugly, you couldn't look at him without gettin' sick to your stomach. I knew a guy that happened to. He threw something in an open fire. It flared up and burned away almost his whole face. He near died from the pain. All the flesh just—''

"Right. Let's get out of here. Galo, tell the lady I have to change the dollars into pesos for her. Tell her she'll get the whole hundred, I promise.''

He translated. She responded.

"She says she'll take the dollars. They are as good as pesos, better, eh? She knows what she is doing, she's a businesswoman.''

Doc counted out fifty dollars. "Fifty now, fifty when we find *cara de cuero*. Tell her.''

Galo obliged. The band burst into song. The crowd dispersed, swarming toward the performers, milling about. They walked back across the plaza to the restaurant. Galo found a corner table by the bar, removed to privacy distance from the other tables, only two of which were taken at the moment. His wife was nowhere about. A pretty young girl had taken over the bar.

"I just wish we hadn't gone and rung the whole town in on this," said Raider.

"Don't worry about it," said Doc. "Nobody knows what's going on.''

"They got to know something is, the way you're throwin' money around.''

"Relax, we're in the homestretch.''

Raider leaned toward Galo. "Miguel, you must be curious about all o' this, so we're gonna level with you. This fella with the mask is the one we're lookin' for most of all. He was a general with the Confederate army, isn't that so, Doc?''

"General Clancy. Very big, very important man.''

"And your superiors in Austin want you to find him and bring him back. To hang him?''

"Oh no,'' said Raider. "Nothin' like that. They just want us to talk to the guy. He's got a lotta information they could use. Bein' a general, he knows a lotta—''

"Rade, cut it out. Let's really level. Galo, listen. We're going to tell you the truth.''

Galo nodded knowingly. "I knew, I knew. I said to myself, Confederate soldiers? Why would they come down here after all these—''

"Will you listen?''

"Of course, excuse me.''

Doc explained their presence in Rosales. Galo listened rapt, without altering his exaggeratedly serious expression; his face said he was having some difficulty putting the pieces together and making sense of the whole.

"But, how will you approach the old man? Without endangering your chief?''

"We'll work something out,'' said Raider. "Maybe hit the house front and back at the same time. Or maybe one of us'll walk right up to the door and knock, while the other covers him.''

Doc eyed him jaundicedly. "Can't you come up with something a little riskier? I can just picture it. They open the door, take one look, and empty a six-gun into your chest.''

"Mine?''

"Galo's right, we've got to put the chief's safety ahead of every other consideration. Wouldn't it be beautiful if Clancy answered the door and behind him was one of his gang with a gun to A.P.'s head? What happens then?'' He paused. "Waiiiiiiit a minute . . .''

Raider and Galo leaned forward.

"Wait, wait, wait, wait, wait . . .''

Raider snorted irritably. "Will you spit it out?''

"The egg lady. She can be the key to the whole thing, the grandson, too."

Galo sobered. "He is not very bright, as I told you, and she is very old. I would not want either of them put in any danger. If something were to happen, it would be very bad. My sainted and beloved wife would scratch my eyes out."

Doc patted his hand reassuringly. "They won't be in any danger. I give you my solemn word on that. If it comes to shooting, they'll be well out of the line of fire. The grandson doesn't even have to be there. Now, follow me. You said she delivers Wednesdays and Saturdays. Tomorrow is Wednesday. Rade, you're about as tall as her grandson."

"I sure don't look like him, thank God. I mean, I . . . I'm not as big, as broad."

"It doesn't matter. You'll be wearing his big hat and his blanket."

"Serape," corrected Galo.

"He rides around with her. He does the leg work, right?" Galo nodded. "When they make a stop, he's the one who brings the milk and eggs to the door. Okay, get this picture, she drives up to Clancy's place. She gets out the order and gives it to the boy."

"Cosme Luis."

"Cosme Luis. Only it'll be you, Rade. You'll go to the door, keeping your head down, the way he seems to like to, so the brim of your hat hides your face. When they open the door, you pull your gun out of the egg basket and jam it against Clancy's stomach."

"Who says he'll be the one answerin' the door?"

"He'll be in the house. He'll show himself."

"You hope. And what about A.P., while all this is goin' on?"

"He won't be in any danger. Once you've got an arm around Clancy and your gun to his head, they won't dare touch the chief. They don't know who you are. You could shoot Clancy down right in front of them. Besides, when you go into your act, I'll be going into mine in the back. I'll break in and cover you. Rade, we've worked it like that a dozen times, exploiting the element of surprise. We'll catch them flat-footed.

"Galo, tell the little girl over there to get us something to eat, would you? Anything."

"Not too friggin' hot," warned Raider. "No damn peppers, please."

"Let's start working out the details."

A tall woman carrying a battered suitcase with two ropes around it, and accompanied by a little boy, came through the beaded curtains beside the bar. She had Galo's eyes, Doc noted, the identical color and setting, but a benevolent Nature had spared her his nose and the pronounced triangular shape of his face. He got up.

"Emmy. Gentlemen, permit me to introduce my sister Micaela Dolores Arango. She has come to visit from Rio Grande in Durango."

Introductions. Señora Arango was going home. Galo's wife came out, joining them. The little boy was introduced; he shook hands with Raider and Doc. He would soon be observing his fourth birthday, Galo informed them. To Doc he looked to be small for his age. His face was wide and displayed an impish grin. His complexion, like that of his mother, was darker than Galo's. Galo pulled him close, pinched his cheek, and mussed his hair playfully.

"Americanos, Pancho."

His sister scowled. She sputtered indignantly in Spanish. Galo grinned and tossed his hand, dismissing her concern.

"His name is Doroteo," he said to Raider and Doc. "Imagine giving a boy a girl's name."

"It is not a girl's!" exclaimed his wife heatedly. "You talk nonsense. It is no concern of yours what his name is." She caught herself, smiling self-consciously at Raider and Doc. "He is mistaken," she added quietly. "It *is* a boy's name."

"I prefer Francisco," said Galo. "I always wanted them to call him that. I suggested it at his christening, but who listens to Uncle Galo, eh Francisco? Pancho is the diminuative of Franciso. Pancho, Pancho."

"*Sí, sí, Tio Miguel.*"

"*Tempo el gusto de presentarle al Señor Pancho Villa!*" exclaimed Galo, again mussing the boy's hair playfully. And sending him into loud laughter. Bringing icy glares from his mother and Aunt Amilamia.

"Francisco Pancho Villa!"

CHAPTER SEVENTEEN

Mama Eufrasia Carlota Hortensia Florentina Moralitos liked the hundred dollars. What she did not like was Doc's strategy. On instructions from both Pinkertons, Galo told her only as much as she needed to know. She protested; she did not want to lose a steady customer. In her narrow view, she could only see Clancy and his associates in terms of Wednesdays and Saturdays, milk and eggs. Over Raider's objections, Doc placated her with an additional twenty dollars.

Attired in Cosme Luis's hat and serape, Raider took his seat in the cart beside Mama Moralitos early the next morning. She delivered to four customers on her route before pulling up in front of a small white farmhouse. Glancing about as she stopped, as he lowered the brim of his hat another inch, Raider oriented himself. They were a short distance from the main road, close to the opposite end of the field he and Doc had seen the farmer plowing the day before. The little house, with its protruding cross beams under the roof, did not appear to go with the field. It stood at least three hundred yards from the end of it on a hillock alongside a stretch of fallow ground. It appeared to be a vegetable garden that, for some reason, had not been planted. Probably because Clancy and his friends had taken over the house, overcoming the owner's objections.

"With a heavy dose o' lead."

"*Qué?*"

"*Nada.*"

They had not come this far in their search of the previous day. Lucky for them they hadn't. If they had and· been

155

spotted, they probably would have been shot off their horses before they got within fifty feet of the place.

The front door beckoned. His initial impression was that nobody was home. He gauged the distance up the slope: sixty to seventy feet. She was getting out eggs, counting them into a basket lined with straw. Under the straw lay his .45, loaded and cocked. He looked ahead. Beyond clutches of agave and cactus a quarter mile distant, oak trees assembled in a small grove. There Galo waited with three extra horses.

His foot touching ground triggered worry. What if old man Clancy didn't show at the door? What if he was sitting in a back room, gun in hand, guarding the chief? Doc, coming up the back, would be able to look in a window, if he could get close enough without being seen. If. What if he couldn't? Even if he was able to, what if he couldn't get inside? The back door had to be locked. He could shoulder through a window. About one thing he was right: They had worked front and back successfully any number of times.

Too many times? Were the odds against success pushed up too high? Was failure overdue?

The earthen jar half filled with milk was heavy. Little wonder the old woman had her grandson helping with deliveries. Raider was now within ten feet of the door. He reached it, setting the basket down, shifting the jar to his left arm. He knocked, bending over, lowering his head, and began pretending he was counting the contents of the basket. The door opened.

Doc rode the pinto at a steady gait, his Winchester roped to the top of his bedroll snugged under the cantle of the saddle within easy reach. He had deliberately taken a roundabout way so that when he came near the house he would be to the rear of it, well out of sight of anyone looking out a window. He would dismount and approach, scuttling through the tall grass the old woman had described when she'd given them the lay of the land. Raider had wanted to ride out so they could see the setup for themselves, but by the time Galo located her again it was late in the evening. It was almost ten o'clock by the time they'd finished sounding her out and instructing her.

The road he had come onto ran northwest all the way to Chihuahua City, according to Galo, whose directions he was following. Putting Chihuahua at his back, he started down it toward Rosales. He would take the first left. It would bring him to the vicinity of the house. It would be to his right, perched on a rise. He would be able to identify it by the agave fence bordering the yard. The old woman had described the exterior of the house down to the last detail, etching a clear picture in his mind.

He picked up the pace. He was leaning over in his saddle, petting the horse's neck affectionately, when it suddenly stumbled and fell forward, pitching Doc headlong. He came down hard.

It was not Clancy who answered the door. Raider did not raise his eyes from his counting, but the voice addressing him was clearly that of a young man.

"About time you showed up, kid, we're fresh out—"

Raider's hand had gone into the basket. Up came his gun, as he jammed the jar into the other's stomach. In the tiny front room Clancy had come up behind the man, his leather mask strapped to his head. He looked weird with only his eyes visible and a narrow slit for his mouth. The man fell back as the jar dropped and shattered, spreading the milk. Raider pushed inside, grabbed a fistful of Clancy's shirt, and pulled him out bodily. Turning him around, he slammed the muzzle against his head.

"Chief! Allan Pinkerton! Come on out!"

The chief appeared in the bedroom doorway at the rear, to the right of the entrance. Behind him a third man showed, gaping like a halfwit in surprise. The man Raider had shoved backwards had recovered his balance and was starting forward, his hand going for his gun.

"Just try it," growled Raider. "I'll blow his brains twenty feet."

Slowly, he backed away, pulling his shield with him.

Clancy had not uttered a sound. Now he spoke. His voice was muffled—understandable, but strange-sounding, as if he were speaking through a narrow pipe.

"You crazy fool. They'll kill ya. They'll cut ya down before ya get down to the road. Shoot! Tobin, Johnny Bob, don't just stand there, damn it to hell!"

"Chief."

Pinkerton came running out, beaming.

"Raider, Raider, Raider."

"You okay?"

"Tip-top."

"Good. Get on down to the wagon. She'll take you down the road. There'll be somebody waitin' with a horse."

He heard a whip crack and the cart start up. Instinctively, he almost turned to look, to yell after her to stop. He caught himself. The man inside staring at him had started for his gun a second time. Raider fired, singing one past his hand. He recoiled, backing away a step, cursing volubly. Once more Raider pressed the muzzle hard against Clancy's temple. And resumed his retreat.

Where the hell was Doc? he wondered. What had happened? Nervous sweat was running down his spine, down his face, a drop stealing through the lashes into one eye, setting it stinging.

"I'll not desert you. Leave you alone with these scoondrals, ootnumbered three to one."

The chief! He had stopped behind him.

"I told you get outta here, goddamn it. Move!"

"Yes, yes."

He could hear him reach the road and start down it, his heavy shoes thumping solidly. Raider cursed under his breath. In seconds he'd be in the clear. Galo would see him coming, bring his horse to him.

I should be so lucky, he thought dismally. Where in red hell was Doc? If he had hit the house from the back as they'd planned, they'd have taken all three by now. Easy as picking apples. Now, all he had was pig one. He'd have to back and back until he was out of range. He stumbled, got his footing, and gripped Clancy tighter.

"Goddamn it!"

"Bit off more'n you can chew, right? Clancy snickered. "Don'tcha dare turn your back, ya' bastard."

"You shut up, I mean it. I'd love nothin' better than to blow you away."

"You dasn't. You need me for cover. You can't hold no corpse up."

"I said shut up!"

Doc lay back on one elbow, drinking air into his lungs, fortifying himself against the sudden agonizing pain. His left shoulder was broken. Had he not twisted his body as he came down, he would have broken his neck. His shoulder had taken the full force of impact. The pain was excruciating, as if somebody were standing beside him pounding his shoulder with a sledge. It pulsed and pulsed and pulsed. He could not move his hand, even his fingers, without sending a white-hot branding iron deep into the break, magnifying the pain almost beyond endurance. Nausea filled his stomach. He was sweating profusely, clamminess stealing over his flesh.

Gingerly, carefully bracing himself with his good arm, he tried to lift then push himself upward, so he could turn into a kneeling position. The iron struck; he cried out. He steadied himself, filling his lungs, exhaling slowly, fighting the nausea, the dizziness threatening unconsciousness.

A sound intruded upon his suffering. A horse was coming up the road behind him.

Following instructions, Galo had departed with the chief by the time Raider reached the trees with his prisoner. The two horses waiting were reined to a branch. He loosed them.

"Mount up," he said.

"Oh, brother, don't make me. Ya can't. I have the god-awfullest time sittin' a horse. It's my back."

"Get on the goddamn horse!" Raider waved the .45.

"Okay, okay."

Clancy mounted as agily as a seventeen-year-old. Lying

bastard, mused Raider, sly as a snake. He'll try anything to delay, confuse, to turn the thing around.

"I live in pain," he whined, "terrible, horrible pain. Burned my face vicious bad. I near died. I hopes to God you'll never have to go through what I did."

"Save it, I'm not interested. And get up ahead o' me. Three lengths, no further, no closer, got it?"

"Okay, okay, you got the gun. And I got the pain. My face, my back, my feet."

"Yeah, yeah, look at me, I'm bleedin' pity. You make one wrong move and I promise I'll kill you. There's nothin' to stop me. Okay, we're headin' back to Rosales."

"Sure, sure."

Where in hell was Doc? he wondered again. They started out, cantering easily, and reached the main road in less than two minutes.

"Hold it," snapped Raider.

He had pulled up. Clancy followed suit. Raider glanced left down the main road, then right. To the right, three hundred yards away, he could see a riderless horse and two men, one standing over the other. A second horse had wandered off into the grass. Even at this distance there was no mistaking its coloring, brown and white.

Doc's skewbald.

"It's got to be . . . Get goin', Clancy. Up the road."

"But you said . . ."

"Do like I say! Move!"

"Mister, you coulda' busted your head. You are lucky."

"I don't feel lucky."

"Must hurt somethin' fierce."

The arrival was young, rugged-looking, solidly built. An ugly scar crossed the top of his cheek under his left eye. He was dirty, dusty; he had ridden a long way. He was trying to grow a mustache, with small success.

"You're Americano, right?"

Doc nodded. "You too."

"Lemme help ya."

"No, no, don't move me. It has to be strapped up. It feels like it's in little pieces." He tried to smile. "I've never felt such pain in my life. Are you heading for Rosales?" The man stared fixedly, his expression vacuous, stupid. "Please stop by Amalamia's. Amalamia's. Ask for Galo. If he's not there, talk to his wife. I need a doctor, somebody who can bind this up properly. Somebody who knows what he's doing."

"Hurts, huh?"

A stupid question, time-eating, unnecessary, thought Doc. Who was he? American. Oh, God in heaven, no.

As it dawned on him it was confirmed. The man had been bending over him solicitously. Now he straightened, his face hardening. He backed away a step. And drew his gun.

"What are you doing?"

"What does it look like? Hey, you want a favor, don'tcha? Want me to fetch help. You got to pay for favors. That's the way o' the world, so my pappy always useta say."

Holding the gun on him, he set about patting his pockets. He found the .38 and jammed it into his back pocket. He found his I.D. He studied it. From his expression it was obvious he couldn't read, evidently couldn't make out a single word. He continued searching him, his hand stopping at the fattest pocket. He grinned.

"Give us see whatcha got there."

"Take it."

He got out Bolton's money. His eyes lit up. He licked his lips.

"Jesus Christ. Oh, man."

"Keep it."

"I got it. 'Smine now."

"Just help me."

"Mister, you don't need no help, you're hurtin' too bad. What you need is to be put outta your misery."

He cocked the gun. The sound of horses coming up the road caught his attention. He looked up from Doc.

"Company. Hey, look, it's the old man."

• • •

Drawing closer, Raider recognized Doc sitting in the road, supporting himself on his elbow. The man kneeling beside him held a gun. Raising it . . .

"Rade!"

Raider's .45 was up, aiming. Bad news, he thought. The other was on the ground, no movement, no jouncing. He fought to steady his iron, to hold his target in the sight. His finger hard against the trigger, he stopped in mid-pull. Doc was too close for unsteady aim. His uncertainty was all the stranger needed. He smirked. He fired. A loud, metallic thud. The gun jumped from Raider's hand.

"Goddamn!"

CHAPTER EIGHTEEN

Allan Pinkerton paced up and down the sidewalk in front of Amilamia's, ignoring passersby, who could scarcely ignore him: His hands clasped behind him, his mumbling, his mounting frustration. He looked very tired; his eyes were bloodshot; he was haggard-looking. His beard had not been trimmed in weeks, and his clothes were rumpled and dusty. He consulted his watch.

"Domn. It's been twenty minutes, longer. He should be here by now. Ond where is Weatherbee? He never showed his face."

Galo stood leaning against the exterior wall. He too was worried. "What shall we do, señor, sir?"

Pinkerton did not answer immediately, did not even lift his eyes. He stopped, turned around, and, shading his eyes, looked up the street they had taken into town minutes before. A woman carrying a washbasket on her head was crossing the street. There was no sign of Raider.

"Domn! We should have waited. He's ootnoombered three to one."

"But they told me very definitely to bring you right back here. They were very concerned for your safety, señor, sir."

"I know, I know. Noo, I'm concerned for theirs. Coom."

"Where?"

"To the police station. We're heading bock oot. We'll need help, five or six capable guns."

"But, Señor Pinkerton, sir, there is only the chief and two policemen. Rosales is small. We are a peaceful people."

"Domn and dooble domn! We've got to get hep soomewhere,

163

ond fast. This delay is oominous. It should not be. Those lods moost be oop to their necks in dootch. We've got to get bock oot. You moost have friends, ocquaintonces, who'd be willing to lend a hond. If it's a question of remuneration . . .''

Galo stared. "Remu . . . remu . . . ?''

"Mooney, mon, *dinero*. You go, get a boonch together. Make sure they're well armed. They'll be paid, ond hondsomely, I give you my word on it.''

"But . . .''

"Coom, show me where your police station is. Three are better thon none.''

Galo raised his hand, pointing. "Across the plaza, next door to Gonzales's *abacería*. Above the door it says POLICÍA''

"I'll speak to the chief. You go. Get your friends. Anybody who con shoot straight. We'll meet by the foontain in ten minutes.''

Confronted with the possibility of exchanging their blood for Allan Pinkerton's money held scant appeal for Galo's friends. Only one yielded to his persuasion, Timoteo Garcilaso Rodriguez, assistant to the local undertaker, a young man who earlier had been among those who had helped restore the wheel to Mama Moralitos's cart. Chief of Police Cortázar also joined them, however, bringing along half of his force: Officer Asturias.

Galo went along. He wore a face that clearly evidenced mingling reluctance and apprehension. But he came. He had willingly helped Raider and Doc, as had Mama Moralitos, before she had fled the field. But to Galo, minding the horses had been without risk, a simple favor to friends who were paying him well for his excellent services, he reflected. Even Amilamia, who found fault with everything, could find no fault with his "arrangement." But confronting the *bandidos* gun to gun threatened bloodshed. His blood. His death? *Madre de Dios*! Had Amilamia seen him riding off with a borrowed rifle with Señor Pinkerton and the police, she would have chased after them. Caught up with him and brought him back by the ears.

They were nearing the hideout. Pinkerton reined his horse to a halt. Cortázar came up alongside.

"They've probably flown the coop by noo." The chief of police looked puzzled. "Cleared oot. Left. Vamoosed."

"*Sí,* you are right, I am sure. Asturias . . ."

"*Sí, Jefe?*"

Asturias was sent ahead to scout the house from a safe distance. They watched him circle it. He came galloping back, pulling up sharply. He spoke to his chief.

"You were quite right, Señor Pinkerton," said the chief. Again Asturias spoke. "They have cut across the fields behind the house. The grass is trampled. And they left the back door open."

"I woonder why they didn't take the road?"

"Through the field would be the shortest way to the Meoqui road."

"Tell him to lead the way," said Pinkerton.

Raider sat on the ground, his hands tied behind his back. He imagined he could still feel the slight throbbing in his right hand, caused by the shot knocking the .45 out of it. What a goddamn eye, he thought ruefully, even stock still and steady as the kid's hand had been.

Clancy had whooped with glee, the muffled sound escaping the slit in his mask. And like that, the tables were turned.

He looked over at Doc. His shoulder was ballooning under his shirt; pain tautened the muscles in his face. The bastards had ignored his pleas, lifted him into his saddle, and forced him to go along. He was in poor shape, getting worse by the minute, not a trace of color in his cheeks. His eyes when he showed them looked dull, lifeless.

They had ridden back to the farmhouse, hurriedly packed their things, and cleared out, cutting across the fields in the direction of the Meoqui Road, according to Tobin, the oldest of the three running with Clancy, and the most intelligent. They were nephews, pressed into service to the old man, or volunteers. At the moment he didn't care which.

They had ridden them a good ten miles. Clancy had spotted

the rocks off to their right and ordered all five up into them to take cover. He stood with his back to the biggest boulder, rising a good six inches above the top of his hat. Johnny Bob lay prone at the base of it, peering down at the road below.

"What in hell we stoppin' here for, Uncle Will?" asked Josiah, the scarred and conscienceless illiterate who had come within two seconds of shooting Doc.

"Use your head, sonny," responded the old man impatiently. "Think." He tapped his own head. "Pinkerton got away, but we got these two, right? He headed straight for town, he waited, they didn't show and they didn't show. What does that mean?"

Tobin interposed. "It means, Josiah, that he figures they've either been gunned down or captured. He figures captured, on accounta we lost him."

"We lost a ace and picked up a couple deuces," commented Johnny Bob and snickered.

Clancy continued explanation. "So the old man rounds up help and comes ridin' back out. He gets to the house, he sees we've lit out."

"Yeah," interrupted Josiah. "Ridin' through the grass back o' the house, leavin' a trail a blind man could follow, Chrissakes."

"Right you are, boy. Which means Pinkerton can follow it. Which means he will. Which means we got him. As good as. We headed straight for the Meoqui road. That's where he'll figure we're headin'." He laughed. "Only we're makin' ourselves a little rest stop. A little ambush." He turned to Tobin. "I purely love this. Always do. Love the surprised look on their faces when they run smack into flyin' lead. Love it, love it, love it!"

"You're not gonna kill Pinkerton." Tobin frowned.

"No, sirree. Gonna get him back. Gonna use these two deuces. That was a good 'un, Johnny Bob, an ace and two deuces. Understan' now, Josiah?"

"I guess."

"Go on with what you was sayin' 'bout Chihuahua City."

"I jus' done like you tol' me. I set round that telegraph

office like a cold toad settin' on a warm rock. Hardly budged. The message come back from Ira up to Lincoln. Governor's gonna hang Lamarr, Clydell, and the rest like he said he was. Set the date for las' week. Only he ain't hanged 'em yet.''

Clancy chuckled. ''I wonder why.''

''I hate to say it,'' Tobin muttered, ''but if we don't get Pinkerton back they're gonna hang, all six.''

''We got these two,'' said Clancy.

''They don't mean nothin', not to that governor. He'll figure these two against six, he's four ahead o' the game.''

''You're right, goddamn his hide, strip it offn' him, and feed it to the hounds!''

They occupied an area roughly twenty by twenty, Raider estimated, surrounded by rocks, ledge, and boulders, perched on the side of a hill forty feet up from the road. Ideal for an ambush. They had hidden their horses up above in a conveniently situated stand of pines. Above the trees were more rocks, studding the slope like barnacles on a ship. Doc groaned.

''Doc . . .''

''You shut up,'' snarled Josiah.

''The man's hurtin' bad, Clancy, Tobin. Can't you help him? Cut away his shirt, bind up his shoulder, take the pressure off the break?''

Clancy knelt beside Doc. ''It is bad, ain't it?'' Doc averted his eyes. ''Shame. But you'll live, 'thout us fussin' over ya.'' He chuckled. ''Live till ya die. Fella, you don' know what pain is. I do. I live with it day and night. 'Scruciatin' pain. Like to split me in two it hurts so sometimes. I got me this salve from a real doctor I put on every mornin', every night. It takes the sting out, but it don't touch the under hurt, the deep down. It's like my skull's on fire under what's left o' my face. Not much, you bet. So don' go whinin' and complainin' to this ol' boy 'bout pain. The little you got you ain't gonna have much longer, take my word for it.''

''Can't you at least bind him up!'' said Raider angrily. ''Goddamn animals!''

Clancy turned toward him. He rose and came over to him. Leaning over, he slapped him hard.

"Shut up. Jus' like you kep' tellin' me to. Mangy bastard. Pickin' on a man twice't your age. Like to pick on helpless folk, don'tcha? That's the way with you Pinks, you're all bastards. That's why I grabbed him, that's why I'm gettin' him back. Big Mr. Law. My boys die, he dies. Let me tell ya somethin', they don' deserve none of it. They're good boys, all of 'em. Never hurt a fly."

Raider was tempted to comment. He held his peace. His face still stung. The man was old, but he was wiry strong. If he'd hit him with his fist he'd have broken his jaw.

Clancy tired of talking. He straightened up. "Tobin, Josiah, gag these two. We don' want 'em yellin' out. One o' you boys might lose your head and shoot 'em. We need 'em till we get him back."

"You never will," said Doc quietly.

Everyone, Raider included, looked his way. His voice was weak, hollow-sounding.

"He can talk," said Josiah, smirking.

"You won't get him back, Clancy," said Doc. "He's too smart for you."

"You think so? He wasn't smart up to Cheyenne when the boys stopped the train. We set the trap, and old lobo walked right into it. And you two with him. Snap, grab, we had him."

"Where is he?" Raider asked. "I don't see him."

Clancy growled in his mask. "I said gag 'em!"

Tobin and Josiah covered Raider and Doc's mouths with bandannas, tying them behind their heads.

"See anythin', Johnny Bob?" asked Clancy.

"Ground and sky, nothin' else."

"Keep watchin', and get your goddamn piece up aside you, so's you'll be ready."

"What are we going to do if we do get him back?" asked Tobin.

"If? What are you talkin' 'bout, boy? We'll get him, you bet your life. Then we'll go find us 'nother place."

Josiah laughed. "Like the first one. That fat little farmer and his wife never knowed what hit 'em. Right, Will?"

"*Uncle* Will, boy. Ya be respectful. And don'tcha be tellin' tales outta school."

Allan Pinkerton slowed his horse and stopped. They had been following the Meoqui road for approximately four miles. Ahead it twisted to the right, and through the trees they could see it straighten. The terrain was hilly, becoming mountainous beyond. Chief Cortázar came up one side of Pinkerton, Galo, the other.

"Señor, sir," said Galo, clearing his throat in preamble.

"May I hov your binoculoors?" Pinkerton extended his hand to the chief. He peered through the glasses, sweeping the landscape ahead.

"While we stand here they are getting away," muttered Cortázar. "They will be in Meoqui in no time. It is only twenty five miles, no more."

"They're not going to Meoqui," said Pinkerton confidently. "They're somewhere oop ahead, mon, laying low, waiting to joomp us."

"An ambush?"

"Oonquestionably. Why else give us a trail to follow, eh?" He lowered the glasses and smiled. "Cloncy *wanted* us to follow him; ergo the trompled gross. He may be a bod opple, but he's not stupid. Nor is he careless. From here oon we've got be extra careful. Ony grove of trees, ony rocks, ony ravine we won't be able to see ontil we're right oop to it, they could be holed oop in. Onderstond, he doesn't want my two ooperatives."

"He doesn't?" Galo beamed. "That is good, wonderful. Sirs, ahem, I have been meaning to ask." Once more he cleared his throat. "It is getting late. My wife expects me at home. Family business. Would you four mind going on without me? I am not a very good shot. I don't even own firearms. I would be more of a hindrance than a help."

"Nonsense!" Pinkerton slapped him on the back in friendly fashion. "You'll do joost dandy. Give yourself a chonce,

mon. You want to get your friends back alive, don't you?
What is it, do they owe you mooney?''

''*Sí*, but . . .''

''Then there you are. We rescue them, you get your money.''

''*Sí*.''

''As I was saying, Cortázar, the lods are of no use to
Cloncy. It's me he needs. Rest ossured, he's oop ahead
waiting.'' He gestured with the binoculars. ''May I keep
these for the moment?''

''*Sí*, by all means.''

''I'm oobliged.'' Pinkerton raised his right arm as if he was
about to lead a cavalry charge. ''Forworrrrrrrd!''

Off they galloped, Galo gradually slipping to the rear.

An hour passed, Raider judged, creeping around the clock
in his mind. Little had changed from the previous hour. The
stinging in his cheek had gone away. Josiah had changed
places with Johnny Bob as lookout. Johnny Bob in turn had
replaced him. Tobin appeared to be exempt from such menial
duties.

''Uncle Will! Uncle Will!''

Clancy ran to Johnny Bob. Raider glanced at Doc. He
appeared to have fallen asleep. He *hoped* he was sleeping.

''Look at the dust comin' up. It's them, it's got to be!''

''I can't see nothin' with these old eyes. Tobin, get over
here.''

Tobin joined them, shading his eyes, squinting. Raider
watched them. It couldn't be the chief. It wasn't possible. He
could smell an ambush six miles away. He'd been a detective
thirty-two years. Knew every trick, every dodge in the book.
Wrote the damn book. The Pinkerton National Detective
Agency, the American Scotland Yard, his brainchild, his
baby. Organized, developed, trained, prepared, and marching
off to war against the miscreant army. The Renos, the Jameses,
the Youngers, the Molly Maguires, the lot. He'd battled and
beaten them all.

He wasn't about to be beaten by some vengeance-twisted,

blood-loving, illiterate sod-busting Jayhawker! With his chickpea-brained kin!

"It's not them," said Tobin sourly "It's a wagon, a farmer. There's no way they'd be comin' by wagon."

Clancy grunted and nodded. Leaning over Johnny Bob, he bellowed, "Next time, hold your goddamn fire, boy! Make certain-sure before ya start caterwaulin'!"

"I'm sorry."

"Sorry dropped the match that burned down the barn that kilt the stock." He glanced toward Raider. "What are ya smilin' at, bastard?" He came over to him. "Laughin' at me, are ya?" Raider mumbled through his gag. "I don' know what the hell you're sayin'; you don' neither. Ya keep a straight face, bastard, iffn ya don' wan' me to burn it offn your head."

"Sun's lowerin', Uncle Will," observed Josiah.

"I can see!" snapped Clancy. "What the hell you expect it to do, sidewise itself? Stupid little shithead."

"Take it easy, Will Francis," said Tobin. "They'll show. They've got to. They know we come this way."

"It's high time they got here. Over two hours since we pulled out. They wasn't *that* far 'hind us. Where the hell are they? You don' suppose the bastard's tryin' to pull a fast one, do you, boy?"

Tobin stared down at him from his superior height, standing a good eight inches taller than he.

"How would he do that?"

"He's tricky."

"You're trickier."

"You sure are, Uncle Will," piped Josiah.

Clancy looked to Johnny Bob for further confirmation. Johnny Bob was not looking his way; he said nothing. Raider pictured Clancy's face behind his mask, what was left of it, the mouth sneering. He was as vain as he was cocky.

They waited in silence. The shadows lengthened, turning from brown to a deep purple, running to the sun descending over the Sierra Madre Occidental. With every passing minute

Clancy got more fidgety, Raider observed, his temper shortening inch by inch, genuine concern rooting itself and flourishing.

"The bastards turned off," he announced at last. "Either that or got lost."

"How could they?" Tobin stared at him in disbelief. "All they got to do is follow the road."

"Could be they never got on it. Never looked 'hind the house. Never did see the grass beat down. Did ya leave the back door open like I told ya?"

"Of course."

"Then they didn' see it. Or the grass. Stupid bastards. Bone stupid! Goddamn, if this don' beat all."

Something, some instinctive force tugged at Raider's attention, got it, and drew his eyes away from the discussion. He looked up the hill at the trees where the outlaws had tethered all six horses. For an instant he imagined he heard a faint, muffled whinnying, but immediately decided that if it were so he was the only one who had. A breeze had sprung up, wandering through the trees, their needles catching the rays of the dying sun, glistening.

His eyes widened. He blinked and strained them. His discovery almost made him gasp aloud: No mistake, it was an arm cradling a rifle, gripping it, aiming downward at them.

"Don't move! Not on inch! You're coompletely covered!"

Four more rifles appeared. Allan Pinkerton emerged. Simultaneous action exploded.

Johnny Bob, lying prone, eyes fixed on the road, twisted about, bringing his rifle up in the same motion. Clancy jerked out his six-gun. Tobin froze, his hand three inches up from his grip. Josiah jumped for the nearest boulder. Firing. An ear-splitting din. Raider threw himself to one side, bringing his knees up in the fetal position, bunching his body as small as he could.

Johnny Bob got off two hasty, wild shots. A single shot from Galo found the center of his forehead.

Clancy stopped four slugs with his chest and stomach before he could aim.

Josiah never reached his cover. His raised left arm exposed

his rib cage. He died twitching, writhing, spitting blood; two slugs had pierced his heart from the side.

Tobin screamed, "I surrender!" Raider heard him. None of the attackers could, over the gunfire. A slug drilled one of his upraised hands. Another struck him full in the face, snapping his head back.

Thin blue smoke rose from the pines, the breeze gathering it in a cloud. Raider swallowed hard. The "battle" had lasted all of six seconds. Down the hill came Allan Pinkerton and his men.

CHAPTER NINETEEN

The four dead had been lined up, their sightless eyes closed, their arms crossed. The ritual position, reflected Raider. Pinkerton clucked disapprovingly.

"Foolish, foolish men, ponicking like thot."

"Tobin was givin' up," said Raider quietly, nodding toward the body alongside Clancy's.

"I saw," said Pinkerton. "I didn't shoot him."

Galo looked away sheepishly. Raider noticed, but withheld comment.

"That happens more'n not when the shootin' starts," he observed, and went back to massaging the feeling back into his wrists.

Doc smiled wanly. "Thank the Lord it didn't happen to . . ." He stopped, his eyes rolling upward. He passed out, falling over on his uninjured shoulder. Pinkerton hastened to his side.

"He's oll right," he said. "He's better off oonconscious with his pain. We've got to get him to the nearest hospitol."

"Meoqui," asserted Timoteo.

Raider was staring at Pinkerton, his expression clearly marveling. "Chief, would you mind tellin' me how in hell you found us? One chance in a million, and you hit the jackpot!"

"Nonsense, lod, it was simple logic—coomon sense coombined with oxperience. One, I was coonvinced beyond doobt thot he wos readying on ombush. The question, oobviously, wos where? Two, ony ombush hos to be set oop beside the road the would-be victims are troveling. One side

174

or the other, thereby ootomotically limiting the choice of sites. Three, pooting myself in Cloncy's shoes, I picked the best possible site.''

He explained that they had deserted the road after traveling it for about four miles. They had gone on parallel to it, keeping it in sight on their right, stopping frequently to study the terrain ahead. He admitted that his strategy was not without some risk.

"We hod a fifty-fifty chonce. They could be waiting for us on oor side of the road or the oother side. The selection of sites would dictate which, eh? Luck wos with us. This spot is to the right of the road.''

Raider frowned. "They coulda bushwhacked you from both sides. It's been done. It's usual.''

"Thot too would depend oopon the site chosen. These rocks were far ond oway the best.'' He pointed to the left of the road below. "We opproached behind those trees, got aroond bock of the hill, ond came oop the oother side. Getting doon to the pines oover the oopen ground withoot being seen wos tooch and go, boot we made it.''

"If they had looked up,'' interposed Cortázar, smiling, "we would have started earlier. Right, Señor Pinkerton?''

"Oonquestionably. Raider, where did you pick oop thot hole in your Stetson? Ond thot livid scar Weatherbee's wearing?''

"We ran into a welcomin' committee just before we reached the Rio Conchos. It got a little thick and noisy for a bit, but no harm done. Not to us, outside o' that crease.''

Doc moaned.

Pinkerton frowned. "He's in bod shape, poor lod. He needs tending to. Chief Cortázar, may we despotch your mon here to the nearest farm to borrow a wogon of some sort? We moost get him to Meoqui the moost coomfortable way poosible.''

"*Sí,* of course.''

Asturias got his orders, saluted, and started up the hill after his horse.

Pinkerton turned to Timoteo. "Señor Rodriguez, Señor

Donoso.'' Galo snapped to attention. "My heartfelt thonks to you both for your assistance. You will be hearing from the agency via the mails." He winked suggestively. He shook Timoteo's hand, then Galo's. "Señor Donoso, if I'm not grossly mistaken it was your occurate shooting thot despotched two of these . . . these conaille."

Galo colored. "Lucky shots, señor, sir."

"Lucky for Ooperatives Raider ond Weatherbee. By the way, hoo mooch do they owe you?"

"Twenty dollars." He pointed at Clancy. "For him."

"Pay the mon, Raider."

"With what? Doc had all the money, and they cleaned him out. That one there, Josiah."

"Thon stir your stoomps; clean oot Josiah."

Raider did so, paying Galo. When Pinkerton saw the size of the wad of bills he whistled softly. And held his hand out. Raider hesitated, and handed it over, explaining where it had come from. Pinkerton smiled broadly.

"If thot isn't irony ot its purest. Think aboot it, gentlemon. These four finonced their oon doonfall, domned if they didn't. Hoo trooly iroonic!"

To Raider's astonishment he then proceeded to peel off a hundred dollars for Timoteo and a hundred for Galo. They thanked him profusely. Chief Cortázar, looking on, licked his lips. Raider almost burst out laughing.

Chief turned to chief.

"Being a pooblic servant, Chief Cortázar, I know you'd never occept recompense for doing your duty. So I'll not tempt you with filthy lucre. Hooever, thot doesn't mean I'm not eternolly grateful to both you ond your mon."

He stuck out his hand. By the time Cortázar finished shaking it, his face had fallen as low as it could, decided Raider.

CHAPTER TWENTY

She pushed her vulva hard against his hand, and his fingers slithered into her warm, slavering quim. She thrashed her head from side to side, her huge, ruby-nippled breasts bouncing. Up came her hips, up, up, pushing, driving. His finger pressed her clitoris. She went wild. Moaning, shrilling, digging her nails deep into his upper arms.

"Take me, take me, fuck me, *fuck me*!"

He mounted her, thrusting his rigid cock forward.

"Make me come, make me come!"

He drove and drove, his spine icing in expectation, his balls exploding, semen spurting, gushing from his cock, flooding her, drenching, filling . . .

"I love you, love you, adore you! It's still hard, a rock, fuck me more! More, more, more."

A loud knocking rattled the door. It struck his ears like thunder detonating.

"Jesus Christ, no!"

"Raider? Oh, Raider. It's me. Are you decent, lod? Hello in there."

Groaning, Raider reluctantly freed his cock from the pool of honey, rising to his knees. The girl gasped, her eyes saucering in disbelief.

"No, no."

"Ssssh, shut up, for Chrissakes."

"Raider, are you alone in there? Onswer me, mon!"

"I'm . . . I'm with a friend."

"Ah-hah. Ah-hah! I might hov known! Hov doon with it,

177

get decent, ond meet me doonstairs in five minutes. Thot's on order!"

"Son of a bitch in a bottle on a stick!"

Decent, Raider may have looked. He did not feel remotely so. Mind and heart were still in bed, loins still between the lady's warm, willing thighs, manhood still engorged by her burning quim. He seethed and fumed and muttered as he descended to the lobby of the Palacio Real Hotel in Meoqui, alloting each one of the twenty-four steps down the two flights its own separate vile word.

Few loungers were about. The desk clerk was asleep at his post, his right ear dangerously close to the attention bell. Allan Pinkerton sat in a capacious chocolate-colored leather chair, an exaggeratedly abused expression separating his hairline and his neatly trimmed beard. Sight of his face would have caused Raider to laugh out loud, had he not been furious. Pinkerton held up his watch.

"You're fifty seconds late."

Raider stifled a growl in his craw.

"What was thot?"

"Nothin'."

"Tsk, tsk, tsk. Yoo're oncoorigible, mon! Rutty os a rooster."

"It's been a long time between waterholes, okay?"

"Con't wait to get yoo're sweaty honds on a señorita ond into the hay for a bounce."

"She's no señorita!" snapped Raider caustically. And immediately regretted it, instantaneously; annoyed with himself for prolonging conversation on a subject that was none of the old man's business.

"She's not?" queried Pinkerton, his left eyebrow rising like a caterpillar on the move.

"She's American," mumbled Raider. "Texas. Come down here to find her husband."

"Is thot a foct? Ond when do you suppose she'll get aroond to looking for him?"

"She didn't say. I figured it was none o' my business.

Sometimes people's business is no business of other people, you know. It can happen. Let's drop it, okay?"

"Ships thot poss in the night . . ."

"What's up? What's so pressin' you got to bust in on me?"

"News, lod, momentous news. Two items, either of which is coonsiderobly more omportont thon your diddling some mon-crazy floozie."

Raider seethed, his lip curling. "I'll be the best judge o' that."

Pinkerton bristled. "See here, mon . . ."

He paused, glancing about the lobby, craning his neck to look past a potted palm at an elderly man sitting, resting his chin on his walking stick, and staring out the window.

Pinkerton lowered his voice. "Let's not get into a domned argument. Joodge this ogainst your infernol lollygogging. I'm hoppy to report thot your partner is recoovering. Splendidly. Dr. Jimenez onforms me his shoulder is knitting beautifolly ond he'll be able to sit a horse by day ofter tomorrow. Boot of course, we'll not soobject him to a soddle. I've made reservations for three places on the stage from Chihuahua City to Presidio." He referred to some scribbling on the back of an envelope. "There'll be stops in Aldama, Coyame, ond Ojinaga, along with the usual rest stops. We con't be too solicitous of the dear lod's health ond welfare, con we noo?"

Raider sighed silently. There were times he could cheerfully wring Allan Pinkerton's neck; there were others when he could throw his arm around him in brotherly affection. The man could be so tight he made every other Scotsrn ın look lavish, but in the hills he had passed out money like a drunken playboy, rewards for services rendered. And his gratitude for their own efforts on his behalf appeared boundless.

He went on. "Secondly, I stopped by the telegroph office on my way bock from the hospitol." He tilted his head, staring reprovingly. "I wos there visiting a friend. You may know the name: Weatherbee. I looked for you in your room before I went over, boot you were oot. Across the street in the contina making orrangements with your playmate, were you?''

"None o' your business. I saw Doc only last night."

Pinkerton held up his hand. "I hod to send my daily dispotch to my dear wife, reossuring her thot I would be bock in Chicago by the end of September ot the latest. Did I tell you thot my son William will be meeting os in Presidio?''

"No. Is that the second news?''

"The second news hos to do with the late Will Froncis Cloncy's offspring. Ot long lost, oll six hove joined their illoostrious father in the great beyond. Hanged by the neck ontil dead, as the joornalists coostomarily term it.''

"Does that suprise you?''

"Not ot oll. Hoovever, I do oppreciate Goovernor Garber's timing. For a while he hod me worried.''

"He never woulda hanged 'em while the old man had you.''

"Possibly, boot occidents con hoppen.''

Raider dropped into the chair beside him, noticing and prudently buttoning the bottom button of his fly.

"Speakin' o' Clancy, you never did get into how he treated you.''

"Tolerobly. The ride doon wos oxhausting, boot once we reached the hoose—which, by the way, hod olready been oppropriated—daily life in his coompany wosn't oll thot bod. Discoonting the tenterhooks. I moost say I breathed a little easier when we got word thot the storm hod knocked oot the telegroph wires between Rosales ond Chihuahua City. Which nocessitated his sending the young one to Chihuahua for word on the stotus of his oonregenerate progeny.''

Pinkerton paused, brightened, snapped his fingers, and pulled out the picture that had graced the front page of *Leslie's Illustrated Weekly*. Given him by Doc, reflected Raider. He held it up.

"Ever see soch a sour oxpression in your life? He's made me look poositively fierce. Noot a trace of the ongrained gentleness ond coompassion for which I'm so famous.''

Raider grunted. "We were talkin' about Clancy.''

"Yes, yes. His plon. It may hov been ill-conceived, born oot of froostration, so to speak, boot as ootlaws go he wos far from stupid. Ond os long os he hod the oopper hond he seemed able to bridle his notural viciousness."

"Tobin was a cut above the lot, even the old man, wasn't he?"

"More ontelligent, perhops, boot noo less inhumane ond rosh."

"Did you and Clancy talk a lot?"

"Hours on end. He never ceased lomenting his sons' plight. To hear him tell it you'd think they wore innocent os babes."

"Did he ever get into what happened to his face?"

"Repeatedly. On overage, ot least once every oother day. He claimed he wos sleeping in a hotel room in Noorton, Konsos. Somebody, he had no idea who, broke in, drenched his face with what smelled like noptha, ond put a motch to it."

Raider reacted, drawing his breath in sharply. "Ever see him with his mask off?"

"Once."

"Pretty bad, huh?"

"Horrible. I looked, closed my eyes, ond nausea blossomed in my stoomoch like a Roman condle bursting. He *wanted* me to see it, wanted me to pity him. Lucky for him I didn't throw oop in his lop. Raider . . ."

"What?"

Pinkerton cleared his throat. "Did I remember to tell you hoo grateful I om?"

"How about me and Doc? We both had one foot in hell till you showed up."

"One foot in . . . Surely not Weatherbee. Ahem, serioosly, lod, ond I'm speaking froom the heart, I'll never forget what you two did, what you went through for my sake, your persistonce, your bulldog determination. Would you believe, oll the time I wos doon there I knew in my heart I could count on you."

Raider grunted. "You knew more'n we did." He was beginning to tingle with embarrassment. "Then too, if we'd played the whole thing a little savvier they never woulda pulled it off in the first place.''

"Balderdosh! I'm os mooch to blame as you two for letting thot greasy little mon into the berth coompartmont so he could oopen the door ond let Bolton in. I, too, blithely stepped oside ond let him saunter by.''

He paused. Somebody was coming down the stairs. Raider took one look. His cheeks flushed and he lowered his head.

"Chrissakes . . .''

"What's the motter? Ohhhhh, I onderstond. Well, I moost say I admire your taste. A fine figure of a woman. My, my. Ahem.'' He leaned toward Raider, his hand cupping his mouth. He lowered his voice. "What did you say her name wos?''

"I didn't. I don't know. To tell you the truth we never got round to names.''

On came the lady, pulling herself across the lobby with her tightly wrapped parasol, the feather in her broad-brimmed hat bobbing gaily, her crinoline skirts swishing. Her eyes roamed. And discovered Raider. And turned to ice. Sniffing, she shot her nose upward and swished by them, waggling her posterior, pushing through the double doors.

Raider sighed.

CHAPTER TWENTY-ONE

November 20th

Dear lads,

I trust you are well, that you, Weatherbee, are completely recovered, and that after your extended sick leave and your overly long vacation, Raider (both with pay, need I remind you), you are ready for a new assignment. You should feel honored, this will be the first time in the long history of the agency that I have assigned operatives a case in a friendly letter, rather than by the usual telegram.

On Monday, November 28th, you will board a train with your ultimate destination to be New Orleans. One G. Esposito, a notorious Sicilian outlaw, is reportedly operating there. He directs an organization which is known in his native Sicily as the Mafia. The agency has been hired by the mayor to assist William's friend, Police Chief David Hennessy, in tracking down Esposito and breaking the Mafia's grip on the city's fruit piers and in the hiring of longshoremen. Upon your arrival in New Orleans, you will report to Hennessy. In line with our policy, however, while investigating, you will be on your own, complementing, but not joining in the activities of the local police. Chief Hennessy understands this and you may expect his full cooperation. Check with him frequently so that you do not duplicate his investigations.

Something of interest to you both. We received a wire from Santa Fe informing us that Artis Henry Thatcher was found guilty of aiding and abetting a capital crime and is now serving a two-year sentence.

Other news on a lighter note, what do you think of our new office typewriting machine? My secretary Mrs. Cookson is delighted with it. It is a Remington. Unfortunately, it cost a thousand times more than a pen, and is as noisy as perdition, but Mrs. Cookson prevailed upon me to authorize its purchase, and I finally yielded to her pleas and blandishments and did so.

Mrs. Cookson also suggested that we equip the office with a telephone. She induced me to try one, which I did at Fenton & Mawber's Insurance Company across the street. Confidentially, I only agreed to try the silly thing because the patent on it is held by a Mr. A. G. Bell, a fellow Scot. I found it a crude device and conversation with the bank on the corner barely intelligible. In my opinion it is a frivolous novelty without any future and, as I informed Mrs. Cookson upon my return from Fenton & Mawber's, there will be no telephone in this office as long as I am in charge.

I trust you received my little gifts. Tokens of my esteem. I shall close now, and once again wish you Godspeed and good luck on your assignment.

Yours faithfully,
Allan Pinkerton

AP:ec

Raider folded the letter and shoved it in his shirt pocket. It was the fifth or sixth time he had read it, doing so repeatedly in the vague hope that the name of their destination might magically change. New Orleans. He spit over the verandah railing of the Sarcoxie Hotel into the dusty street. He had never been in New Orleans, nor had he the remotest desire to go there. Fixed in his mind was the conviction that it was a pesthole, the Delta's answer to Chicago. The only city he had ever seen worth the money it took to get there was San Francisco.

Doc hailed him from across the street, waving his free arm, the shoulder of the other still in a cast. He was sitting a big bay, holding the reins of Raider's horse near a hitch rack. Raider waved back, adjusted his gift from Allan Pinkerton—a brand-new Stetson—at a jaunty angle, picked up his bedroll and saddlebags, and descended the steps, spurs jingling.

At least they would be traveling to New Orleans in style, he mused, on horses. They had plenty of time; it promised a leisurely ride. Forget the train. He had had his fill of noise and rattling and cinders. Besides, on the way down they'd be slicing through Arkansas, God's country, much better seen from a saddle than through a grimy, yellow window at forty miles an hour.

"It's about time," said Doc as Raider came up to him, flung his saddlebags over his horse's rump, and set about tying on his bedroll.

"What's the grand rush?"

"It's almost noon." Doc produced his brand-new Waltham watch, the gift of Allan Pinkerton. "We should have been on the road hours ago."

Raider mounted. "You're like a kid with a new toy. You gonna haul that thing out every ten minutes all the way down?"

"Why not? It's a beauty. It's also the most amazing thing that's ever happened to me."

"What are you talking about?"

"Rade, this watch is the gift of the stingiest man in the Western Hemisphere. When I opened the box I almost passed out from shock. Seeing that card with his name on it . . ." He smirked. "Don't tell me you weren't just as surprised and pleased when you got your new hat. Which reminds me, you told me you'd never give up your old one."

"I didn't say that. What I said was I'd never have it cleaned."

"You threw it away?"

"Man, I had to. It had a hole in it. A hole in a Stetson can be dangerous. When you're nappin', and you got it pulled down over your eyes, a bee, a hornet, a horsefly, buffalo gnat, anything packin' a stinger can fly inside and attack you. Insects are nosy as hell, you know."

"Sure."

"I love this hat. Man, it's aces full. It's got to be the most expensive one old J.B. makes. Doesn't it look great on me?"

"How can you stand the smell of brand new?"

"Wiseass."

The wind came up, roiling the dust, lifting it into spinning wraiths. It tousled the horses' manes, whipped dust into Doc's eyes, set a nearby store sign swinging, creaking loudly, and snatched Raider's hat from his head. It landed and began rolling on the edge of the brim.

He swore, jumped from his saddle, and hit the ground running. "Come back here, goddamn it!"

The hat outdistanced him with ease, crossing the street diagonally, teetering and toppling to rest upside down. Against the hind legs of a mule. It did not turn its head to see what had struck it so lightly just above both fetlocks. Instead, it raised its muzzle and emitted its customary feeble hoarse noise in resentment. It could have easily kicked the hat clear with either hoof. But nature called, giving it other ideas. . . .

Sarcoxie was two hours behind them. They had forded the Kansas River and passed through Eudora. Raider continued sulking. He talked to himself in low, indistinguishable tones. He sputtered and fumed and seethed and growled and grumbled. He cited the unfairness with which the average man was confronted at every turn over the course of his lifetime. He called down the wrath of the gods on all mules "and their filthy ways." His hand kept going to his hatless head.

Doc took all he could before finally capitulating.

"Rade, for God's sakes, why didn't you retrieve it, wash it out in a horse trough, and have it cleaned? No, forget that, strike it out. Why didn't you stop in Eudora and buy a new one? Why? Really? Or is it that you have your heart set on subjecting me to this all the way to New Orleans? All the way back. From this day forward. Is that it? Is it?"

"It's not fair."

"I know! I agree. Unfortunately . . . Look, tell you what. The next town we come to, we're going to find a men's store, we're going to stop, and I'm going to buy you a brand-new Stetson. I don't care what it costs.''

"Five dollars."

"Whatever. Think about that, Look forward to it. Your problem is solved."

Doc slapped his reins lightly against his horse's flank and rode on. Raider galloped to catch up.

"Doc . . ."

"What now?"

"I just wanted to say. Five dollars is a lotta cash, so, well . . ."

"It's all right, it's all right, it's worth it!"

"I just wanted to say, I'd be more than willin' to pay half."

Doc turned to him slowly, staring in astonishment and disbelief. Raider nodded. Doc rolled his eyes heavenward and, looking off toward the horizon, shook his head and picked up the pace.

Author's Note

On page 153 Francisco Villa is introduced. Villa was born Doroteo Arango in Rio Grande, Durango, to Agustín and Micaela Arango on June 5, 1878. In 1890 Doroteo's father died of tuberculosis. At seventeen he killed a landowner for abusing his younger sister. Outlawed, he took the name "Pancho" Villa, after a well-known bandit of an earlier day.

Villa headed a well-organized rustling ring in the northern states. Beginning in 1909 he became deeply involved in revolutionary activities. On March 9, 1916, he led some four hundred men across the border in a raid on Columbus, New Mexico, killing sixteen people and partially burning the town. The next day President Wilson ordered a force into Mexico to capture Villa and his men. The expedition failed, and three months later the Americans withdrew.

Villa remained under arms until 1920, when the Mexican government purchased his retirement with the gift of a large estate. On July 20, 1923, his car was raked with rifle fire, and Villa and three companions were killed.